TOONAMINT
of Champions

How LaJuanita Mumps Got to Join
Augusta National Golf Club Real Easy

"If it's wacky you want, it's wacky you'll get with Toonamint."
ForeWord Reviews

If it's wacky you want, it's wacky you'll get with Toonamint of Champions, Georgia humorist Todd Sentell's spoof about a golf nut's lifelong dream to putt around the Augusta National Golf Course, and, as a bonus, have his non-golfing hairdresser girlfriend, LaJuanita Mumps, pinned as "the first ever" female member of the Club.

Where else but in Sentell's bubbly imagination could a kooky hero like Waymon Poodle from Mullet Luv, Georgia rise to the top? A constant daydreamer with one blue eye and one green, his office is located "right by the condom and genital lubricant counter" of a busy supermarket. He's so addicted to golf he rents only apartments numbered 1931 to commemorate the year Bobby Jones debuted at the Augusta Masters. His bedroom replicates the course, and, believe it or not, he prefers golfing to giving up his virginity to LaJuanita despite her come-ons. To complicate the comedy, Waymon's duffer of a supervisor is also named Waymon, which leads to several convoluted conversations reminiscent of Abbott and Costello routines. Toss in Poodle's paranoia about Giant Cicada Killer Wasps and their impending take over of Augusta's famous twelfth hole—despite the attempts of entomology professor, Jeevpil Biswapati, and his flamethrower—and you end up with a "toonamint" even the Marx brothers would roll their eyes at.

Sentell's nine years as "the director of sales and marketing for an ootsie-tootsie private golf club" gives him the background material for carving up golf's sacred rituals and icons of the greens. His expertise as an established humorist has him operating with wit and polish. The problem with humour, though, is that what tickles one man's funny bone may aggravate another's. Some readers may find the raunchy fondling between Augusta's 79-year-old receptionist, Betty Simpson, and 42-year-old head accountant, Frank Johnson (aka Emiglio Rafsooliwicki) not as hilarious as the author had hoped. Others may shy away from our hero's abortive attempts to cover up Betty's Bermuda Grass when she hikes her skirt to give Chi Chi Rodriguez a peek at her private turf. On the other hand, Waymon's volunteer position— position number 1931, by the way—as "Manager of the Rope at the Practice Facility Invitee Entrance and Exit," and his round of golf with The Golden Bear lead to moments of universal fun. His initial telephone conversation with Rafsooliwicki is true classic comedy, while the episode of his orange jacket among all the green jackets in the Augusta Club's dining room is Masterful satire.

Regardless of which way your funny bone swings, Sentell's Toonamint of Champions will give a brand new meaning to "par for the course." M. Wayne Cunningham/ForeWord

TOONAMINT
of Champions

....

**How LaJuanita Mumps Got to Join
Augusta National Golf Club Real Easy**

A Particularly Allegorical Comedy of Real Bad Manners

....

TODD SENTELL

READ THIS BOOK.

Join shit.

Todd Sentell

KÜNATI

TOONAMINT OF CHAMPIONS

For information, contact Kunati Inc., Book Publishers in both USA and Canada.
In USA: 6901 Bryan Dairy Road, Suite 150, Largo, FL 33777 USA
In Canada: 2600 Skymark Avenue, Building 12, Suite 103, Mississauga, Canada L4W 5B2,
or email to *info@kunati.com*.

FIRST EDITION

Designed by Kam Wai Yu
Persona Corp. | www.personaprinciple.com

ISBN 978-1-60164-005-5   LCCN 2006930186
EAN 9781601640055   FIC016000 FICTION/Humorous

Published by Kunati Inc. (USA) and Kunati Inc. (Canada). Provocative. Bold. Controversial.™

http://www.kunati.com

TM—Kunati and Kunati Trailer are trademarks
owned by Kunati Inc. Persona is a trademark owned by Persona Corp.
All other tradmarks are the property of their respective owners.

for ERROL SANDERS

Who got all this started. In 12th grade.

Acknowledgements

The author thanks the following people for their friendship and support during the writing of this book: Jeff and Feryal Hendricks, Susan Sanders, Jack and Joan Sentell, Stuart and Margaret Conrad, Bradley Dunckel, Denise Gibby, Stephanie Lipnick, Sally and Danny Hood, Don and Grace Sentell, Ed and Gloria Rego, John Companiotte, Bruce Fraser, Warren Grant, Randy Waldron, Jeff Paton, Shannon Bower, Ronnie Musselwhite, Doug Hollandsworth, Dondra Hedden, Mary Grace Stubbs, Cheri Riley, Victoria Sanders, Sara Daniels, Robert Youdelman, Frank Curtis, Ed Thompson, Charlotte Raines, Glenn Sheeley, Vern Johnson, Ellie White, Pat Sykes (a dang good bank teller, too), and the man who organized the toonamint, my publisher, Derek Armstrong, Kam Wai Yu for his amazing designs, and my brilliant editor, James McKinnon.

I also want to thank two little rascals named Landers and Jackson, who forever wondered what daddy was typing, and why he was always laughing so wildly, sitting there all by himself. They wanted me to read a bunch of the book to them. Ain't no way.

And to their beautiful mother, Susan. Thank you.

"This would be a great club if it weren't for the goddamn members."

A post-consulting pronouncement by Zoran Geckstein, a distinguished private club management consultant, on a number of notable American golf clubs

There are psychologists who believe that in playing golf man is in a way reverting to the primitive, that striding over the course, occasionally searching for the ball and then hitting it, reproduces, in mild form, the hunting life and activities of the savage man. How they square this with the hundreds of thousands of women who play golf, I do not understand!

from Bobby Locke on Golf, *1954*

"I wouldn't go *near* a golf course."

A women's rights agitator

PART I

Relentless Obsessions

From the March, 2007 issue of *Go Figure,*
the monthly report of the
American Psychological Association

———————————

*In conclusion, we weren't real surprised to find that
every teenage male human on earth concocts frantic sex
fantasies for fifty-six seconds out of every waking, sleeping,
and comatose minute. Their thoughts during the other four
seconds range from the outcome of professional and collegiate
sporting events to the condition of their zits to how to get their
parents to buy them a BMW.*

*However, we also found that middle-aged male humans
concoct frantic sex fantasies, but for only one second of
each minute. Their thoughts during the other fifty-nine
seconds of each waking, sleeping, and comatose minute,
relentlessly obsess about how they might get a tee time
at Augusta National Golf Club.*

And then there's the women.

Old Mrs. Willard

WAYMON POODLE IS A TELLER at the Trust Trust bank branch inside the Publix grocery store on Confederate Victory Parkway in Mullet Luv, Georgia, and no other human being on earth loves more than he does the Masters, the golf course on which it's played, the wonderful sport of golf in general, and the iniquitous allure of what goes on behind the gates of ootsie-tootsie private golf clubs. No one. Not even Jack Nicklaus.

Waymon constantly dreams of one day, somehow, some way, getting to play Augusta National Golf Club if LaJuanita Mumps, his new fiancée, was okay with him being gone for most of a Saturday or a Sunday or a Monday or whenever the miraculous morning or afternoon or whenever the miraculous moment happened even though she articulated in Waymon's face, a lot, that she thinks the wonderful sport of golf in general and the iniquitous allure of what goes on behind the gates of ootsie-tootsie private golf clubs are for flaming squids, bald fat farts, and mules.

"Mules" is the mean and awful word LaJuanita calls women. She knows it's mean and awful, but that's just the way LaJuanita feels since she deals with women and the hair on their head or their upper lips or on their nipples or in their armpits or down there between their fat legs all day for six days a week, so she says to everybody that she's justified. "Here comes that *mule*," LaJuanita says when she sees her customer and the customers of the other hairdressers get out of their pickup trucks with their cigarettes in their mouths, still eating something.

"Iniquitous" is a word Waymon and LaJuanita learned in Sunday school.

Anyway. So Waymon dreams.

Constantly.

No other word comes close to describing Waymon's obsession with his thing: unrelenting, skull-exploding fixation, perhaps, but that's four words.

For example, a very regular customer at Waymon's bank branch, Old Mrs. Willard, wrote Waymon's branch manager, a couple of days ago, a letter. In the letter she said that when Waymon serves her lately she's pretty dang sure that he's not concentrating on his work and if Waymon doesn't seem to care for her business that she would come and get all her money from TrustTrust and go give all her money to them people over at the BB&T, which was actually closer to her vein clinic, her dead husband's grave, the Pontiac dealership where her sister works the cash register in the parts department, and that new Super Wal-Mart where you can buy food, so that tells you something about how much I love Waymon Poodle. Old Mrs. Willard underlined: can buy food, so that tells you how much I love Waymon Poodle.

For instance, Old Mrs. Willard wrote that two weeks ago she gave Waymon a check to cash for $250, given to her by her brother-in-law for something personal, and she was always thankful, by the way, that in all these years Waymon never asked her why her brother-in-law gave her money for something personal. Anyhow, Waymon gave her back $82,000! Old Mrs. Willard underlined $82,000! four times. She wrote that TrustTrust should thank the Lord God Jesus that she was an honest Christian martyr because she immediately, without Satan's greed consuming her old body and soul, made Waymon aware of his mistake. And even when she made Waymon aware of his mistake she thought she might have gotten a better reaction. Plus, he's been giving me those big fat orange lollipops that taste like my colon polyp medicine. I done told Waymon exactly ninety-two times I don't like those kind of lollipops because they taste like my colon polyp medicine, but he keeps on giving them to me. It's like he's all of a sudden from some outer space planet standing there looking at me with that eye of his. But please don't fire him, she wrote, as I truly think in my heart Waymon's a fine young man and a dang good bank teller. I really do. Old Mrs. Willard underlined eye and dang and fire, one time. Colon polyp two times, in the second reference.

The branch manager, who was also named Waymon, went to Waymon at his teller window with Old Mrs. Willard's letter in his hand and right in front of a valued customer who was supremely enjoying being served by Waymon, waved the letter, limply, back and forth, but with a perceptible level of obnoxia, and then moaned, "So... day *dreeeeeaming* about playing Augusta National Country Club for the one hundredth billionth *time?*"

"Golf club!" Waymon squawked. "*Golf* club!"

It was well known.

Worshipping Satan

Waymon immediately remembered what he was thinking about when he accidentally gave Old Mrs. Willard an extra $81,750. And it made him feel good: it was how he would play the par three twelfth hole, also named "Golden Bell," if he ever got a chance to play Augusta National Golf Club.

Waymon knew that Jack Nicklaus, who had won six Masters beginning in 1963, said that the twelfth hole at Augusta National Golf Club was the hardest par three in the world in championship competition. So if Jack Nicklaus thought this about Golden Bell, then Waymon knew in his heart it was true. Actually, if Jack Nicklaus marched up to Waymon at the bank branch, and instead of initiating a banking transaction asked Waymon to gouge his eyeballs out with an ice pick and worship Satan, Waymon, even though he was a type of Baptist called "Primitive," and could speak in "tongues" when he got all emotionally riled up, would immediately march to aisle seven where the ice picks are sold and gouge his eyeballs out and worship Satan. Just because Jack Nicklaus told him to. Right there in aisle seven.

It was the calm, quiet Monday after the Masters. Waymon had daydreamed as he flipped through the cash drawer for Old Mrs. Willard's money, and all the pin placements he saw on TV the previous day were the same and it was sunny and about seventy-nine degrees, just as the announcers said when the telecast started on Sunday. All the trash and half-chewed-up pieces of pimento cheese sandwiches people spit onto the grass had been cleaned up and the TV cameras and those awful TV tower things and the concession tents were long gone too.

During the night, all the bunkers on the golf course had been cleaned out and filled with new sand and raked to a consistency like Dixie Crystals. Plus, Fuzzy Zoeller and Tiger Woods were in a twosome ahead of him, just out having a nice time, swapping socially acceptable racial jokes and making birdies and eagles and holes in one and laughing and walking down the fairways of Augusta National Golf Club without all the patrons drinking alcohol-based beverages and pointing at them. And in a threesome behind Waymon were Arnold Palmer, Gary Player, and Jack Nicklaus doing the same thing: out having a nice time at Augusta National Golf Club, something that happens naturally after you drive through the gate. Actually, earlier, on the practice range, Jack Nicklaus had marched up to Waymon and complimented Waymon on his swing. Jack Nicklaus said Waymon's swing was, for a non-professional, the greatest swing—technically and aesthetically—in the *world*. This brief interaction with the greatest golfer who has ever lived made Waymon really happy.

Waymon had also been assigned the best and wisest caddie at Augusta National Golf Club and the caddie had been reading Waymon's putts real well for the previous eleven holes. So real well, in fact, that all Waymon did was place his Titleist Scotty Cameron "Newport" putter behind the ball, then say to the caddie in his most business-like tone, "Tell Waymon what to do." Waymon never argued with the caddie and was planning on giving him a big tip.

The caddie had also been complimenting Waymon on his swing and never once seemed to mind that he was asked to take a picture of Waymon holding his golf bag on every tee and by every green and when Waymon insisted he pause in front of a number of landscaped areas and clumps of azalea bushes that were particularly memorable.

When the caddie complimented Waymon on his swing, which was after every swing, the caddie would say, "Good *swing*, Mistah Poodle."

Then, because Waymon knew the caddie to be wise, he would look the caddie squarely in the eyes and say, "Yes. I'm nutting it today here at Augusta National Golf Club."

"You surely *is* nuttin' it, sir. *Surely* is," the wise caddie would say to Waymon.

And the wise caddie would also say to Waymon—about a million times. "You surely is rollin' yo *rock* today, *too*. Rollin' that rock."

"Thank you," Waymon would say in return—softly, reverently, with his eyelids half closed in near exaltation, to the wise caddie. "Thank you very much for noticing."

Hole after hole, Waymon thought: Oh, Lord God Jesus, how incredible it was to be finally walking on the other side of the ropes. Sometimes he would say "Oh, Lord God Jesus" out loud as he gazed at the incredible blue sky watching over Augusta National Golf Club. Oh, Lord God Jesus.

Waymon was six under par as he stood on the twelfth tee. Remember to look at the top of the pine trees behind the green. Waymon, of course, remembered. Waymon knew that the wise caddie would, by the twelfth hole, instinctively know his game. He knew that by that time the caddie would know exactly what club to give him as he stood there looking at the flag on the historic twelfth green, flapping lazily, with his right arm extended toward the caddie and his ball freshly rubbed with a wet towel and his white tee—one of a handful grabbed out of a wicker basket in the pro shop—shining so brightly in the Augusta sun.

He knew that when he nestled his 6-iron behind the ball, something wonderful would happen: a little butterfly would twitter around the ball, then light upon it. A butterfly. A little yellow one, innocent, never in harm's way as he sat on the golf ball of Waymon Poodle.

Waymon would watch the butterfly open and close its wings as it sat on the ball, Waymon's favorite type of golf ball, a Titleist balata, 90 compression. Waymon loved the way the black Titleist lettering and the red number looked on the ball—so dang professional. He knew at that instant how he would explain the greatest moment of his entire life to his friends he played golf with at the Mullet Luv Golf Center.

He would explain it in rich, somber detail.

He knew he'd probably even tear up.

Using his 6-iron as a support, Waymon leaned down to gently brush the butterfly away so he wouldn't kill it at impact, and reached out with his gloved left hand (FootJoy, white, medium) and took back the enormous wad of money from Old Mrs. Willard and became unnerved by the odd expression on her face and wondered for the millionth time why in the world TrustTrust would put a branch office in a noisy supermarket right by the condom and genital lubricant counter.

Flop Shot

But Old Mrs. Willard was right.

Waymon was a fine young man and was indisputably proven—revealed every year of his employment by the massive TrustTrust customer survey—to be the friendliest and most competent of any teller in any branch in all five states and the District of Columbia in which TrustTrust did business. But for some reason, no one at TrustTrust ever told him.

"How are *you* today?" he'd chirp in a tone of voice, however squawking, that was unequivocally unconditional in its sincerity, no matter if Waymon knew the valued customer to be annoying, stupid, a fornicator, morbidly obese, foreign, gross, fraudulent, or really smelly—or all of those things in one. They were still the valued customer. And he dang loved them.

And when the transaction was complete, no matter how difficult or how long it took, he'd squawk, "My name is *Waymon* and it was a pleasure serving *you!*" Waymon then, on purpose, as the valued customer walked away, would reach over and move his nameplate in the direction of the valued customer so they would remember him. Then he'd quickly turn the nameplate toward the next valued customer as he called out (squawked), "Waymon's here to help our *next* valued TrustTrust customer to-*day!*"

So screeching was Waymon's squawking that valued customers would scrunch up their shoulders and make expressions as if they heard a cell phone go off at a funeral. But Waymon never noticed.

Couple this remarkable customer service with the way Waymon looked: Waymon looked faintly similar to how aliens are described by those who insist to Larry King on TV that they've been abducted and taken to outer space and had their anuses probed with big tubes by the aliens. Big eyes. Big head. Long skinny arms. Long skinny fingers. A scalp of blond fuzz, but when the light hits it a certain way it looks a little orange.

Important to mention, too, is that Waymon's eyes are exotropic. In other words, the left eye points one way and the right eye points way out the other way. And once a person gets to know him they still have a hard time dealing with it. Plus, one eye is blue and the other one is green. So Waymon is what anthropologists call a one in a million human being.

It should also be mentioned that Waymon's banking career didn't begin at the Publix. It began at the TrustTrust freestanding branch, right down the road, also conveniently located on Confederate Victory Parkway where they had him work the drive-through window most of the time. After Waymon's first few weeks there were collisions by customers into the support poles and into the two ATMs and into the air shuttle machines in the drive-through area and other tie-ups as most customers would not immediately drive off after their transaction was complete. When they did drive off, they usually weren't paying attention to their driving one bit. A number of loyal customers were finally compelled to say something although new business increased. One even took a picture of Waymon from his truck and e-mailed it to a Mullet Luv radio station. Certainly the citizens of Mullet Luv loved having TrustTrust in their community, but were compelled by Lord God Jesus himself to tell the branch manager and the police who came to handle accident scenes, and to break up fights between the drive-through window area loiterer-gawkers who were starting to congregate every Monday through Saturday afternoon, that it was like watching a freak show... even though it's un-Christian and uncouth the way we've been carryin' on... pointin' at it... but you just cain't look away... what with that fucker from outer space on the other side of the window, flapping around in there and talking at us through the intercom. So TrustTrust had transferred Waymon to the Publix branch, where he now thrives professionally.

And that's it, really, unless Waymon's intimate psychological, fashion, sportsmanship, automotive, and coital-related particulars are fascinating and unusual and odd and have absolutely anything to do with Waymon ever in his life playing Augusta National Golf Club.

The Particulars

The Intimate Psychological Particulars

Waymon was so profoundly afraid of giant cicada killer wasps—not just any kind of wasp, as there are many kinds of hymenoptera, but the giant cicada killer wasp, who sports a pulsating yellow and black thorax and a long stinger—that a Christian psychologist he finally consulted on his giant cicada killer wasp situation labeled Waymon "insectophobic," specifically concerning giant cicada killer wasps and told him, under no circumstances whatsoever, to daydream about them. Or, if encountering one, never to reach out with your hand, gloved or otherwise—even if you've got your golf glove on and one gets on your golf ball—and try to flick a giant cicada killer wasp away. Just run off real fast. Six female giant cicada killer wasps got into Waymon's car in 1998. Female giant cicada killer wasps, of the two sexes, are the more aggressive. The windows of Waymon's car were closed and were of the manual type. Waymon drove his car through a McDonald's dining room and into, and around, for five minutes, as his brakes were now not working anymore and the accelerator was stuck, the new car lot of a Porsche/Ferrari/Bentley dealership. When it was all over, the police and the paramedics and the firemen and the general manager and the top salesman and a guy still clinging onto Waymon's windshield wiper who'd been eating an Egg McMuffin, and four potential customers of the Porsche/Ferrari/Bentley dealership found Waymon grasping, very tightly, his steering wheel, speaking in tongues. A paramedic had to pry Waymon's fingers off the steering wheel with a screwdriver as Waymon was experiencing a cadervic spasm even though he was alive.

After further pondering Waymon's situation and discovering that there were no giant cicada killer wasp support groups anywhere in the world, the psychologist browsed the Internet and found two web sites completely devoted to giant cicada killer wasps. The psychologist was amazed that anyone would care enough about some freaking *bugs* to develop web sites about them. She nonetheless suggested that as part of Waymon's therapy he consult these two web sites as often as he could stand it and to possibly, one day, appreciate giant cicada killer wasps as God's creatures too, as he was one as well. She thought that might appeal to Waymon, her saying "God's creatures." She said it a lot when she talked to him. It didn't appeal. Okay. The Christian psychologist said he could read about, on those web sites, what turns out to be their fascinating pupation habits and safely gaze at giant cicada killer wasps in color photograph form on a computer screen. Think that might help? Pupation habits? Praise Jesus?

Shakily, wearily, and with extreme tension, Waymon said he'd give it a try. But he told her CompuServe always took a long time to come up.

The Fashion Particulars

At the bank branch, Waymon wore only white, short-sleeved, button-down, 100% polyester dress shirts until TrustTrust issued a company-wide memo saying that long-sleeved dress shirts, for male employees, were more appropriate in the work place since a number of you people should not bring attention to yourselves. Waymon never knew he was the one that forced the memo. He has long, freakishly skinny, pale white arms that seem to flap everywhere when he talks or when he swings his golf clubs.

The ties Waymon wore when he first started at TrustTrust were the most anonymous ever sold by Sears in the history of the company as Sears was his favorite place to shop for clothes as many of the male salespeople there reminded him of himself and this made Waymon feel welcome. But one day, when Waymon ordered through the Masters web site an Augusta National Golf Club logoed tie, which has a green background covered with little Augusta National Golf Club logos, he began wearing it to work every day and to church every Sunday. It's a tie people notice. But Waymon has to endure from his so-called friends at church and from a large number of valued TrustTrust customers upon noticing the tie, this repulsive question: "Oh, *Way*mon, so you're a member of the Masters?" Waymon, as his patience was constantly tested by this query, has to explain, in his squawking voice, that a person isn't a member of the *Masters*, that that's the *tournament*. A person would be a member of Augusta National *Golf* Club. That the Masters is the tournament they have at Augusta National *Golf* Club each year in April. Waymon will then make sort of a huffing sound, similar to the huffing sounds made by three-year-olds.

Plus, when valued customers, from time to time, appear at his window with a Masters-logoed shirt or sweater or jacket, it makes Waymon's heart race. Sometimes a Masters-logoed wallet or money clip. One time a valued customer was wearing a gold signet ring with the Masters logo engraved into the ring. When Waymon saw it he about fainted.

The Sportsmanship Particulars

Waymon never cheats at golf, even though his golf buddies at the Mullet Luv Golf Center do, and, unlike these people, Waymon never shoplifts boxes of balls and drivers and shirts and golf bags and umbrellas out of the pro shop when the assistant pro is helping somebody else or playing video poker.

Waymon prays at Waffle Houses before he starts in on his food without feeling embarrassed one bit, even when the waitress is standing right there with more iced tea. Waymon loves iced tea, sweet. With nine lemons.

The Automotive Particulars

Waymon changes the oil in his car's engine every two thousand miles, as opposed to every three thousand miles. Waymon's car, the one he bought after his fender bender, was a green (for the Masters) 1978 Chrysler "Diplomat." He would have bought a Volkswagen "Golf"—sure, an obvious choice—but Waymon buys American. Waymon loves America. Waymon believes in wearing a car out before you get another one.

The Coital Particulars

Waymon was proud that he met LaJuanita at one of those church watermelon socials where everybody ends up squirting each other with Silly String, and not at a bar or disco or rock concert or adult video/sex toy store, although Waymon would never go to a bar or a disco or a rock concert or an adult video/sex toy store anyway, even though there are four adult video/sex toy stores within easy walking distance right next to the apartment complex where he lives in Mullet Luv.

Although LaJuanita oozes frantic sex fantasies, in a caked-on makeup sort of way, and when her hair is real huge and fluffy looking and when she has on all of her rings and has all of her earrings inserted, and sometimes when she wears a fake diamond-studded choker, Waymon was proud that he had not yet fornicated with her although he was hard at work currently denying the temptation to fornicate with LaJuanita even though LaJuanita said it was all right to fornicate since they were definitely getting married. *Hell*, LaJuanita says, there's somewhere in your *Bible* that says it's okay to fornicate all you *want* if you're officially engaged—but Waymon knew she was lying. He knew the Bible. After they got married, LaJuanita was planning on keeping her last name so she'd stay LaJuanita Mumps as opposed to LaJuanita Poodle.

Anyhow, a lot lately, LaJuanita was attempting to dial up a sex channel, available for $12.95 for a six hour "Sex Attack," on Waymon's local cable television provider in hopes that seeing other people for six hours—however attractive or unattractive or sex-mixed—in the act of love making would arouse Waymon to fornicate.

Waymon, of course, wrestled the phone out of LaJuanita's hands before she could successfully place the order. Plus, he's always watching his favorite channel, The Golf Channel, when LaJuanita grabs the channel changer and tries to change the channel to get the 800 number for the Sex Attack because she never can remember—except for the 800 part—the number for the Sex Attack.

So Waymon courageously denies LaJuanita's attempts at fornication, as well as sexual acts on a lesser degree than fornication, with a biblical strength of will not to be believed, such as when, late in the evening three days ago, as Waymon and LaJuanita were the only folks in Waymon's apartment clubhouse hot tub, LaJuanita, on purpose, let her left titty flop out of her bikini top. LaJuanita's titties are the size of pink grapefruit. LaJuanita was hoping Waymon would scoot over there and gnaw on it. It was glistening with hot tub water, the titty, and she was holding it up with her hand and was winking at Waymon and her nipple was as red and inviting as a cherry. Waymon gazed at LaJuanita's titty and thought of Augusta National Golf Club… and it suddenly occurred to him that he might be the only person—the only *golfer*—in the world who really enjoyed pondering the original names of some of the holes while he was driving to work or sitting in a hot tub with his woman. One hole name Waymon thought was a dang *vine*. Waymon suddenly felt the urge to work through them… right… okay, now… "Pink Dogwood" used to be "Woodbine"… *that's* right… and "Tea Olive" used to be "Cherokee Rose" and Waymon remembered that "Pampas" was called "Cedar" and he smiled when he remembered that "White Dogwood" used to be called just "Dogwood" and by gosh ol' "Chinese Fir" used to be called "Spanish Dagger" believe it or dang not, and then Waymon sort of snickered when he remembered that "Three Pines" is now called "Golden Bell." But Waymon was still gazing at that shimmering huge left titty of LaJuanita's. And LaJuanita was still holding it up... and still squeezing it and still winking at him because she was real horny for Waymon. She could just imagine what it would be like. Them two really going at it like they were on drugs... like they were part of some government experiment. Right there in the greasy bubbles of the hot tub... steaming wet sexy Waymon action... especially if another hot, sexy couple like them came walking up and wanted to get in there with them. Waymon unconsciously winked back at LaJuanita... and thought about how he'd play the par three fourth hole at Augusta National Golf Club, Waymon knew to be originally called "Palm," now called "Flowering Crab Apple," traditionally one of the hardest holes for a Masters' titty.

Invitee.

He'd hit a 4-iron. Smooth.

The Mantra of Portent

So such was the level of Waymon's particular focus on his thing.

Looking at him, a person new to Waymon would immediately, without an instant of giving him the benefit of the doubt, consider him to be a flaming squid, potentially dangerous, a serious ectomorph. Hard up. Haunted.

Maybe.

But could drop anytime and do one hundred without stopping. Ran a marathon once, just for the fun of it, in tennis shoes and swim shorts. Arm-wrestle him and get yours wrenched off at the elbow. Is always sweet to LaJuanita and somehow understands that she thinks the wonderful sport of golf in general and the iniquitous allure of what goes on behind the gates of ootsie-tootsie private golf clubs are for flaming squids, bald fat farts, and mules. Actually, LaJuanita makes him nervous and Waymon tries real hard not to show it. Waymon would be a perfect Marine, except for all the profanity he'd have to use. Waymon loves the music of the Carter Family, especially any song that includes Mother Maybelle Carter. When she sings, it makes Waymon's skin crawl and his hair stand on end. Her intonations also send chills up Waymon's spine. Waymon likes an occasional movie, too. Listen to Waymon imitate his favorite movie star, Ernest P. Worrell, and it'll make your skin crawl and send chills up your spine and make your hair stand on end just like Mother Maybelle does him.

But he's not a loser either—or those other things. Focused as a red laser beam Waymon is on his thing. Prepared to lose his woman over golf. Prepared to die in his quest to play Augusta National Golf Club if he has to, gladly. Waymon Poodle, prepared to squawk at Death, "Sir, I've caught up with you on the twelfth tee of heaven on *earth*, which is called Golden Bell at Augusta National *Golf* Club. Let *me*, Waymon Poodle of Mullet Luv, Georgia, play through, and we'll have a Coker-Coler in the men's grill after our round of golf and talk about my appointment with *heaven*."

Death, most likely in a sarcastic tone of voice because Waymon figured he brokered more souls for Satan than Jesus, would snarl at Waymon, "We won't be talking about *Hell*, Waymon? You're *sure*... absolutely *positive*...

Waymon Poodle won't be going to mother fuckin' *Hell?*"

After taking a real deep breath, Waymon would squawk at Death: "*Yes.*"

Waymon Poodle of Mullet Luv, Georgia: suffering from something.

Of course. Waymon had thought many times of how his life would turn out if he never got to play golf at Augusta National Golf Club and this was a horrifying thought.

The thought made his brain squirm.

Made his heart race.

His lungs suck for air.

Waymon's dreams, nearly every night, thoroughly deal with this topic, in multi-color.

All this makes him a little self-absorbed, Waymon.

In other words, in Waymon's mind there are two distinctly different types of people in the world: those who have played Augusta National Golf Club and those who have not played Augusta National Golf Club.

In a hazy, faraway place, where screams echo, Waymon saw the two groups float around in monstrous hoards, dressed in white robes, naked underneath, but wearing FootJoy golf shoes with SoftSpikes, and the ones who had played Augusta National Golf Club had satisfied expressions on their face and enjoyed lives that were finally worth living. Now they went forth and prospered and finally cured all the people in the world who had colon polyps.

The ones who had not played Augusta National Golf Club spewed things from out of their mouths that were not nice. These horrifying people drooled and giggled and screamed and reached through the clouds and touched each other's private parts with their fingers and lips and allowed giant cicada killer wasps to crawl around on their hands and up their arms and up their necks and onto their faces without even trying to knock them off—not one bit.

So Waymon prayed, mantra style, for fifty-nine seconds of each minute, that the Lord God Jesus would see fit to place his name on the Augusta National Golf Club tee sheet and on a guest list with the guard in the guardhouse on Washington Road.

Waymon asked the Lord God Jesus to drive him through the gate after the guard saluted him and told him—Mr. Waymon Poodle of Mullet Luv—how nice it was to have him as a guest today and hopefully many,

many times in the future.

Waymon, then, with the Lord God Jesus' assistance, would drive slowly, reverently, desperately trying not to run over all those weird looking magnolia pine cone things on the asphalt of Magnolia Lane, then into the locker room, to lunch in the men's grill, into the pro shop to say hello and to thank them and to buy seventeen logoed shirts, onto the practice range, then onto the first tee of Tea Olive. Amen. Corner.

Refrigerator Gone

Waymon believed in omens. Especially omens that directly related to him getting to play Augusta National Golf Club.

Not that he couldn't think for himself—obviously, he could, in quite imaginative ways—it was just that Waymon needed incessant confirmations that his dream to play Augusta National Golf Club was valid and the tremendous mental energy and prayer time he'd been investing all these years would not make him look goofy.

In Waymon's case, his most recent omen's message was truly undeniable. And when the omen was revealed to Waymon, even under the horrible circumstances, Waymon breathed, "Thank you, Jesus. You are the man."

What happened was this: Waymon's apartment was sanitized. Burglarized, as in sanitized. Wiped real clean, as in burglarized by professionals.

The two guys who did it, a Mitch and a Ken, while staking out Waymon's apartment complex a few days before the break-in, couldn't help but notice the bug-eyed, creepy-looking motha-scratcher in the beat up Diplomat whose comings and goings were as predictable as they'd ever seen in their combined twenty-two years of robbing people's homes, apartments, businesses, out buildings, lake homes, beach homes, detached garages, attached garages, mountain homes, Dempsey Dumpsters, basements, warehouses, self-storage garages, pontoon boats, cars, and sport utility vehicles. They had also once wiped out two coolers of sirloins at an Omaha Steaks in Gourd, Arkansas and ate like restaurant critics for three and a half years. So they had seen the business thoroughly.

Anyhow, here's how predictable Waymon Poodle was to Mitch and Ken, the burglars. Wednesday night, since Waymon didn't sing in the choir—but was thinking about auditioning for the tambourine—Mitch and Ken quickly discovered that Waymon would come home to his apartment at exactly 7:39 in the evening, always covered in sweat and with his hair all wet and matted. This was his night to hit two large baskets of range balls with his friends at the Mullet Luv Golf Center. And like all places called golf "centers," it consisted of a baked-out, divot infested nine holes you play twice from two different sets of tees, a practice range (lighted) with hard-packed dirt and Astroturf mats, a pro shop that sells the worst stuff and a grill that serves those ubiquitous orange crackers, hot dogs, beer and iced tea, and one brand of cigarettes, Marlboro Lights. So here he comes, Waymon Poodle. And there he goes inside with his golf clubs slung over his shoulder. Saturday morning: out the door with his golf clubs slung over his shoulder at 7:45 a.m. and back at 6:03 p.m. Sundays: church, lunch, etc., etc., etc.

After several days of watching Waymon, Ken said to Mitch that it seemed like the motha-scratcher was *taunting* them. That the motha-scratcher probably *knew* they were casing his motha-scratching ass and that he was probably a motha-scratching FBI agent or some *other* motha-scratching shit. Ken would get madder and madder as he pondered this scenario, while hitting himself on the forehead with the butt of his pistol.

Mitch, the more reasonable of the two, lit yet another cigarette and didn't say a word so he would look cool to Ken and continue to dominate the relationship as the mastermind and whatnot. After a moment, though, and after having been bugged by something for years, Mitch very politely asked Ken if he'd quit saying motha-scratcher and instead might he consider saying "motor scooter" as motor scooter was a bit more socially acceptable when a person had to talk like that. Plus, saying motor scooter was sort of funny and really caught people off guard when they thought you were about to say motha-scratcher and actually helped you make your point more effectively in an oddly humorous way.

Ken looked at Mitch in disbelief, and then said in an unequivocal tone of voice that there was no motha-scratching *way* he might consider saying motor scooter instead of motha-scratcher. And then he said to Mitch real tough, pointing his pistol at Mitch's eyeball, "And *when*, motha-scratcher, did you turn into a wimpy person?"

Ken was going to stick his pointing finger into the end of the barrel like he had seen the James Garner character do in that cowboy movie he loved a lot, but all of a sudden Ken began banging the butt of his pistol onto his forehead again. After about a minute and a half, he finally knocked himself unconscious.

So, of course, as is quite common to interpersonal relationships of this nature, Mitch knew that one day he'd have to slit Ken's throat and shoot him in the head.

Anyhow, on a Monday morning three weeks ago, forty-five minutes after Waymon left for the bank branch, Mitch and Ken rid Waymon of every possession he owned except the items contained in the second bedroom.

Here's the scene: Mitch and Ken moving everything out of there in a hurry, with sweat pouring off their faces. Like two movers.

A resident of the complex, a former New York Mafia kingpin type, who, after a quick career change decision, had his whole head resculpted to look like a retired Clark Gable impersonator, who was in the FBI's witness protection program, who lived near Waymon, who was out walking his Chihuahua with one of those electronic leash devices that include a shock button to make the dog stop running away or leaving a shit where it's not supposed to, said to Mitch and Ken to wish Waymon well and that he'd miss him.

Cordially, as if they'd been trained by Letitia Baldridge herself, Mitch and Ken said they most certainly would and to have a good one.

So Mitch and Ken stole everything, everything. Except the contents of the second bedroom. Which included a brand new computer that could have fetched some serious motha-scratching cash. But they didn't steal it.

As Mitch and Ken also believed in omens, especially real bad omens, they immediately knew their motha-scratching asses would be cursed if they so much as breathed on any of the shit in that room. It was just the way the whole motha-scratching thing was set up. Spooky as motha-scratching *shit*.

The Second Bedroom

Waymon's apartment number was 1931. For a real big reason.

Everybody who loves golf like Waymon knows that 1931, the year, was when Bobby Jones, the founder of Augusta National Golf Club, first set foot upon the land that is now Augusta National Golf Club.

Of course, folks even more like Waymon know that Bobby Jones really preferred to be called "Bob." Waymon always had to explain this to people once he got real agitated at them when they said things to him in conversation such as, "You know, *Waymon*, ol' *Bobby* was one of the greatest golfers in the *world*," and "You know, *Waymon*, ol' *Bobby* learned to play golf at East Lake Country Club while he lived in a *mule* shed or some such," and so on and so on and so on. Waymon would then make that huffing sound. At that point more like a two-year-old, which was worse.

Anyhow, five years ago, before Waymon moved out of his parents' trailer, he called every apartment complex in Mullet Luv, asking them if they had an apartment numbered 1931 and was it available and did it have two bedrooms. The first complex he called said yes they do have an apartment number 1931 and it's available and it has two bedrooms and the second bedroom even comes with a nice view of a dumpster. Waymon looked at the phone in his hand: *Dang*, an omen.

Nonetheless, here's what Mitch and Ken saw after they opened the door to the second bedroom in Waymon Poodle's apartment number 1931 in the Sans Souci apartment complex in Mullet Luv—which strictly prohibited a resident from painting or wallpapering the walls or the ceiling— on the Monday morning they cleaned him out: Old Bob Jones' Spalding golf clubs, with the yellow enamel-coated shafts, were laid across the five blades of the ceiling fan and hanging off every club was a set of old leather, plastic, or nylon head covers. Mitch and Ken discovered this almost instantly because Ken turned the light switch on so the fan started up on "high" and all that motha scratching shit got flung everywhere which really, really startled Mitch and Ken and made the whole scene even scarier.

Every golf magazine ever sent to Waymon in his life was stacked against the left wall of the room with the spine facing out so Waymon could easily check the date of an old issue for some obscure golf tip when he got on the bogey train.

The magazines were stacked to the ceiling, and because there were so many magazines in the room, the room had that old, musty odor found in libraries and the dark homes of shut-ins. Waymon subscribed to a lot of golf magazines and because of this he secretly thought that at golf magazine conventions he was talked about by the publishers of these magazines. It was just a thought, but Waymon could not believe that anyone else in the world went to the lengths he did to find and to subscribe to golf magazines. Waymon even subscribed to a number of foreign golf magazines such as *Golf Russia*, *Golf & Piss* (Ireland), *Hooking in Cabo Del Sol*, and a Japanese golf magazine, whose title, when translated into English, was *Mashie Niblick Tennis Genitals*, and even included full page pornography. Waymon was amazed, gazing a while, at how little the Japanese people looked without their clothes on while they fornicated, but then he'd rip those pages out of the magazine and throw them away. U.S. Open, PGA Championship, British Open, and U.S. and British Amateur Championship programs were also sent to him.

But Waymon's all-time favorite golf magazine came out only once a year and that was the *Masters Journal*, distributed just a few weeks prior to each year's Masters. The fact that it was available in the magazine rack at the Publix in which his bank branch was located wasn't a big omen, but it did rate as a pretty good one.

Waymon couldn't wait to get his hands on it each year and had even made an agreement with the produce manager, who was also in charge of receiving magazines, that he be allowed to come back there at the loading dock and be the first one to cut through the plastic adhesive tape on the box and reach in and get the first one. The agreement, however, had to be vigorously explained and renewed each year as the turnover rate among produce managers at the grocery store was extremely high and Waymon also learned that most people who are produce managers don't quite understand these types of sentiments and tend to forget them the second after Waymon went to the trouble to explain them.

Waymon loved to gaze at the cover photograph of his *Masters Journal* issue as it always showed a hole at Augusta National Golf Club with the sun shining so brightly on the sixteenth… the thirteenth… the whatever… it didn't matter to Waymon if they showed an exploding commode as long as it was an exploding commode at Augusta National Golf Club. Seven dollars for so much pleasure. Each page for Waymon was an oasis of golf and Masters information. He would turn the pages slowly, and each re-reading was just like the first, slow and respectful of all this thing meant to him.

And the heft.

The heft of the magazine was so impressive to Waymon, unlike any of his others, those with thin pages and all those dang ads that showed half naked people.

The *Masters Journal*, read with his eyes wide open. Waymon forgot the world existed, didn't hear the phone ringing, knocks at the door, his stomach grumbling. Up until the final putt of that year's Masters, the magazine would rest on his night stand beside Waymon's Bible.

Which they stole.

Mitch and Ken stood there still gripping the door frame, wide-eyed themselves, as if the door had opened to reveal an open elevator shaft.

Mitch kept sucking on that cigarette.

Clickety-Clack

On the far wall were two windows. Their drapes: golf hole fabric. Like pajamas.

Under the window was an old office credenza Waymon had bought for $3 at a yard sale and the top was covered with various Masters knick-knacks, all logoed—ball repair tools, ball markers, money clips, tumblers, mugs, scarves, scorecards, coasters, the whole motha-scratching shooting match—he'd purchased at the only Masters he ever attended, 1988, (the Monday practice round actually; the only ticket he could get) and other golf knickknacks people had given him. Waymon was easy to buy for. People felt sorry for him.

On the wall to the right was Waymon's collection of golf books displayed in shelves Waymon built himself that stretched to the ceiling and ran the length of the wall. Every golf book ever written by Bob Jones and O.B. Keeler and every other person on earth who had ever written a book on golf or the Masters or Augusta National Golf Club was on those shelves.

Waymon's golf bag full of Nike irons and woods—just like Tiger plays and some of those other pros—leaned against the shelves. His head covers had Masters logos on them.

All of a sudden Ken said "motha-scratcher look at *this* shit," and that scared Mitch half to death as for some time the mood of the burglary had been somber and quiet. Ken pointed to the center of the floor. On the floor was Waymon's masterpiece, his unabashed most prized possession in the world other than his love of the Masters, the golf course on which it's played, and the wonderful sport of golf in general. On the floor was Augusta National Golf Club. In miniature. To say how and how long it took Waymon to make the model and how possessed he's become of it was fairly depressing—just to say that every acre of Augusta National Golf Club, including the par three course, the 18-hole course, the cottages, employee parking, the maintenance center, the garbage dumpster, everything, was created in such detail that it took Mitch and Ken's breath away. Ken wanted to say motha-scratcher, but couldn't.

A small light placed in the corner of the room by Waymon shone on the clubhouse. Waymon kept it on all day and all night, for he wanted there to always be light on the clubhouse of Augusta National Golf Club.

To their left and right, the walls were covered with framed prints of Augusta National holes. Amen Corner. The clubhouse. Bob Jones. Jack Nicklaus. Coody. Palmer. Hogan. Hord Hardin.

The walls, what you could see of them: Masters green. Augusta National Golf Club green. Pantone Matching System number 560. Waymon had the solution memorized. Seventy-two point five percent green, seven point five percent of warm red, and then you throw in exactly twenty percent black. Or you could look at it this way, he'd explain to you if you were still listening: you got fourteen and a half parts *green*, one and a half parts warm *red*, and four parts *black*.

Masters green.

Five. Six. Zero.

Waymon knew in his heart that it was the green that was the best.

The Future

Back to the omen.

Waymon had come home at exactly the time he comes home on Monday and inserted the key into the lock and opened the door to apartment number 1931.

Waymon stepped into an empty apartment. He stood there in the living room for a moment, not quite gawking but almost, then stepped back out and looked at the number on the door, you know, just to make absolutely sure. Seeing the number—1931—immediately made Waymon feel good as that was a big year for golf.

He closed the door, took a deep breath, then opened it again and stepped into yet again an empty living room and experienced a feeling of vulnerability. And that's what he felt. Vulnerable. Like a kitten. And Waymon didn't like feeling this way as he secretly thought people shouldn't mess with him. But there he was, and someone had messed with him.

Without moving, he viewed the devastation and wondered what might be revealed to him when he looked into the second bedroom.

Seeing the future, Waymon knew, from watching a certain episode of *Star Trek*, could make you go insane.

The Conspiracy

The first thing the Mullet Luv policeman said to Waymon, as he gazed into Waymon's second bedroom, was, "Mr. Poodle, I assume you must be a member of the *Masters*."

At that moment Waymon knew once and for all that a conspiracy had been developed and the conspiracy was organized in an effort to mess with him because you aren't a member of the Masters. The Masters is the tournament they have at Augusta National Golf Club. This he explained to the policeman.

Well, the policeman articulated, he had never given it that much thought.

Meanwhile, an unfortunate turn for Mitch and Ken, at least from their point of view. Two hundred and fifty miles down the road, the huge U-Haul truck they had rented with a stolen credit card which they used to rid Waymon of everything he owned, except the contents of the second bedroom, blew up. In addition, it happened to blow up and catch on fire right in front of one of those regional Georgia State Patrol center places, as U-Hauls will do whose back ends drag on the asphalt for over one hundred miles at high speeds.

In Georgia, as well as in a lot of other states in America, as state patrolmen are trained to do, they ran out and came to the aid of the motorists in the U-Haul with the engine area engulfed in orange and red flames. Mitch, as he quickly exited the U-Haul, forgot that his gun was still stuffed into his pants and that most of the gun was still hanging out and it was pretty damn obvious to these well-trained state patrolmen that what was sticking out of Mitch's pants was a gun.

This, of course, didn't go over real well with the state patrolmen and Mitch was quickly notified of his particular situation. Ken, still exhausted from the move, was sleeping, and didn't get to see Mitch have to fling his gun down, which he had actually purchased with his own money, which he had stolen, and get it all scratched on the asphalt, then get enthusiastically gang-tackled by seventeen state patrolmen.

Anyhow, Mitch and Ken and the U-Haul were brought back to Mullet

Luv where criminal punishment precedent was set. As part of their punishment, because the local authorities just thought it was logical and made sense, Mitch and Ken were uncuffed then forced to haul all of Waymon's shit back into apartment number 1931 to be placed in exactly the same spot where his shit was before. Waymon and Mr. Gable, holding his Chihuahua, watched patiently from the parking lot.

When they were finished, Mitch and Ken got cuffed again and hauled off. Before they were hauled off, the Mullet Luv policeman said tentatively, with an edge to his voice, now that he thought he might be speaking to a lunatic, "Mr. Poodle, good luck with your omen situation." Then he left, fled, quickly.

Waymon thanked Jesus, performing a clogging step he learned in church revival camp. He looked as if a bunch of giant cicada killer wasps were attached—by their claws and stingers—to his ankles.

Friends Like These

Such was Waymon's confidence in the omen, he couldn't wait to tell his friends on Wednesday at the Mullet Luv Golf Center. He really should have known better by now.

These particular fellows, who found irresistible only one thing about Waymon, his golfing, made great sport of him in nomenclature form. They called Waymon "Waymo" or "Way Off" or "Sideways" or "Wide Angle" or "Squidward."

Because of Waymon's alien likeness situation, they absolutely delighted in calling him "The Experiment" or "The Mistake" or "The Unexplained" or "Spock" or "The Chicken" and a real favorite was "The Insect."

"Hat Rack" and "Pool Cue" and "Flag Pole" and "The Javelin" because he was so skinny, and from time to time they referred to him as "The Tendon."

They also called Waymon the "Missing Link" and deeply believed in their hearts that he was the world's official Missing Link and that they had discovered it right there, living and working in Mullet Luv, and had befriended it. However, there was a special nickname they called Waymon, which was surprising in its conception by folks considered to be hillbilly-type dumb asses, since it had a cinematic, literary quality to it. In other words, a human being had to be fairly alert to come up with it. Waymon's Mullet Luv Golf Center pals called him, on special occasions, "Nosferatu." Amazing their depth of cruelty, from a literary point of view.

They also made fun of his Bible thumping. The way he talked. But his north Georgia twang was just like theirs.

They told him how he'd never get promoted at his job because he was so much like Barney Fife. Now, how Waymon reasoned his future they especially loved. They hooted and hollered and pointed back at him. Clickety-clack. Clackity-click. But he beat their asses in golf and took their money on the eighteenth green then slipped it back under their windshield wipers.

Breaking 80, and sometimes 70, was real easy.

Waymon hit golf shots that hissed.

But Waymon's mission was his wall. It was brought down between himself and outside forces attempting to dissuade him from believing that he would tee it up one day at Augusta National Golf Club. Now he knew he would, but he didn't know when. His friends, after the golf ball whacking, tried to help.

THE SCENE: the snack bar at Mullet Luv Golf Center. Many beers. Iced tea for Waymon, sweet. Cigarette packs lying next to lighters. Smoke everywhere, thick as vanilla yogurt. They're sitting around the big, round table, its yellow plastic top pock-marked by years of cigarette burns.

THE PLAYERS: Waymon, who was "Nosferatu" this evening, and two rurals—"Snort," who two weeks ago, while worshipping Satan, gouged his left eyeball out with an ice pick, and Billy, an enthusiastic Cane Toad licker, best friends—and a nice guy named Jim who was real educated and had clean fingernails and clothes. Billy and Snort drunk before they got there. Getting drunker. Shirley, the sweet country gal who worked behind the counter. Her hair done up, black and shiny, like Patsy Cline. She loved Waymon and thought how Waymon was just exactly like Jesus when Jesus was Waymon's age. After a couple of vodkas, Shirley thought Waymon might *be* Jesus. Shirley loved Jesus, very much, but smoked, drank, cussed, and kept a vibrator in her pocketbook. Used it quite a bit through her tight jeans behind the cash register. Shirley loved a rocking orgasm.

SNORT: "Dumb ass Nosfera-*tooo*, that's the biggest crock of shit story I ever *heard*. Them fuckers didn't have any more goddamn *room* in the goddamn truck fer yer *Masters* shit."

NOSFERATU, bony finger, wagging it: "I *seen* in the truck. I done told you. They had *room*."

SHIRLEY, whiskey voice, Southern accent out of Hollywood: "Y'all leave him *aloooo one*. And quit calling him that awful *vampire* name, you Satan worshiper assholes! Now I *mean it!*"

BILLY burped, a piece of something flew out and hit Nosferatu in the corner of his eye.

SNORT, slowly, with malice dripping from every word; strange, rubbery facial expressions: "Aw-right. Here's the *deal*. See, since them *dooods* didn't take off with yer precious *golf* shit, now you think that any goddamn second some fart wad *member* of Auguster National *Country* Club is gonner prance up to you on the goddamn *street* and say Nosfera-*tooo*, since them fuckers didn't take any of yer *golf* shit, I just feel like *you*, Nosfera-tooo Poodle, a freak from outer *space*, ought to come on down there with *me* and make *me* look like a *dumb* ass in front of all my other member assholes and suck on a goddamn *hot* dawg and play *golf*? I mean, give me a fuckin' *break*. *Kill* me… just fuckin' *kill* me, *maaaaaaan*."

The group, except for Nosferatu, let go a tremendous burst of laughter, as if on cue. Laughing so hard their faces turn red. Devil red. High fives. Low fives. They're pointing at Nosferatu's face. Knew they got him good with that one. Cigarettes sucked in so hard their cheeks collapsed. Another high five. Funny, funny stuff. The way it was delivered by Snort—just awesome. The tempo. The facial expressions. The empty, weeping eyeball socket. The way he leaned into Nosferatu's face and kept screwing his head sideways as if he were looking under a sofa for his roach clip. Awesome. Plus, plus. Not done yet…

SNORT: "And hey, Nosfera-*tooo*. If you really, really look at that Auguster National logo, the bottom of that flag don't come out nowhere goddamn *near* Auguster, that goddamn flag looks like it comes right outta Spartanburg, South Caroliner, or some *other* hell hole from out of my *butt*. Boy, you just look at that low-go and tell me I… ain't… *right*!" Snort falls off of his chair and breaks his collarbone, but he keeps laughing because he doesn't feel it.

Awesome. Creeped the *shit* out of him.

Shirley started having an orgasm. Then her cell phone went off in her pocket. The extra vibration. Shirley fell on the floor and started squirming around and had the rest of her orgasm down there.

NOSFERATU, jaw clenched so hard his cheek muscles popped to a visible point. Jesus on his side. Praying again, mantra style: "I'm gonner tee it up at Augusta National. I know I'm gonner tee…"

JIM didn't know how he got pulled into the group, seeing as he was a big shot regional vice president of IBM, but just always happened to be around on Wednesday afternoons. Loved to hit balls for cheap, and found out pretty quick this was what you got. This scene. People who will definitely fuck with you, without permission. But sort of understood the Waymon situation as he had a brother like Waymon whose life mission it was to marry Barry Manilow. The restraining order came last Thursday.

But Jim was laughing too: "Nos—I mean *Waymon*, you know, there are some ways to play Augusta National without being invited by a member."

SNORT AND BILLY, as if on cue: "*Bull* shit." A palm-smacking high five, with the broken collarbone. Loud. "Fuckin' A *maaaaaaaan*." Then a low five. Loud too. Smack! They had it down, but couldn't do it sober.

NOSFERATU knew this was what hate felt like.

JIM waited for total silence: "*Waymon*, look at me—"

SNORT AND BILLY: "*He caint!*"

SHIRLEY: "Y'all leave Jesus alone!"

JIM, holding firm, needed to get this over with: "I know you know the qualifications to get into the tournament, Waymon. I'm sure you've got them memorized."

NOSFERATU, tapped a finger on the side of his enormous head.

SNORT AND BILLY, leaning in so they can hear.

JIM: "You don't think you'll be going over there and winning the British Amateur anytime soon, do you? Although you're a great player—don't get me *wrong*."

SNORT, nudging Billy: "Nosferatooo, you *are* a great golf player. You really are! You go over there and win yer-self the goddamn British *Oh-pen!*" Laughing. Laughing like hell at that one. Trying to catch their breath. Holding their throats.

JIM: "Waymon, *you* know what I'm trying to say."

NOSFERATU, wide-eyed, mesmerized. Didn't say a word. He knew.

JIM: "And I bet you saw that article the other day in the *Wall Street Journal* about Bill Gates and how he wants to join Augusta National. Loves golf. Seems like a pleasant enough guy. The richest son of a bitch computer geek booger eater in the universe. The shit he invented has given millions of people around the world opportunity and made whole economies and made our worthless lives easier. You saw the article. He wants the fuck in there and he licked their asses *big* time and those boys told goddamn Bill Gates to back up slowly down Magnolia Lane and hit the *road*."

NOSFERATU: "Okay, then. I saw it. I *read* it." The profanity, Waymon thought. Does everybody at IBM cuss like that?

JIM: "I knew you'd find it somehow. You're a magnet for that shit. But, Waymon, if they won't let Bill *Gates* be a member, that just shows you how hard it is for some regular stiff like you to just *play*. Well, I mean you're not regular at *all*, Waymon, you're special."

NOSFERATU: "I've been *told* that." Nosferatu gave Snort a look.

JIM: "All right then, here's the deal. There are exactly four ways regular stiffs can play down there. They let the golf writers play the day after the tournament, or you can work there at the club and there's an employee day once a year, or you can get a job as a volunteer during the tournament and they let you play on a day near the end of the season. Other than *that*, you have to be invited by a member. No offense Waymon, but I don't get the impression you know a whole bunch of Augusta National members. Bill *Gates* sure as hell ain't one, we know that."

SNORT AND BILLY, gaping mouths. A spooky quiet. Spooky calm. Cigarette smoke slowly pouring out of their nostrils like white ropes. They never knew what to say when this Jim cat befriended Waymon like this. At some point every Wednesday night Jim did—had to. This Jim fucker had class. Fuckers with class scared Snort and Billy shitless.

JIM, with an exhilarating hopefulness in his voice, a squeeze of Waymon's bony shoulder, and a life-altering wink: "Waymon, *amigo*. Those four ways and you're on the first tee at Augusta National Golf Club looking up the emerald fairway of *Tea* Olive. I'm pretty sure."

PART II

Waymon's Void

Removing a Wart

Lay down your bet if you thought Waymon got any sleep that night. Darkness enveloped him like a casket and he couldn't wait to get rid of it so he could get rolling again.

Waymon didn't sleep. He squirmed.

Waymon's plan was to get a real good job in the accounting department at Augusta National Golf Club as soon as possible.

Although Waymon thought he might be a good waiter at Augusta National Golf Club, since he really enjoyed serving people, but then he knew he'd be serving folks alcoholic beverages, and drinking alcoholic beverages or being the person serving them, was a one-way ticket to You Know Where.

One thing was certain; Waymon Poodle wanted to be an employee at Augusta National Golf Club right now. Nothing else would do. He wanted to work there every day of the year. Wake up in Augusta, Georgia. Live in an apartment there, number 1931. He wanted his business card to say Waymon Poodle, Accountant, Augusta National Golf Club. He could see this clearly in his mind—his Augusta National Golf Club business card, as big as a billboard, hovering there in front of him.

For lunch, Waymon and all the other tellers got thirty minutes. Waymon wanted an extra ten. He was going to hustle back to his apartment and call Augusta National Golf Club from the second bedroom and get a job in the accounting department then hustle back to his old job at the bank branch and resign real quick and start packing. He'd figure out what to do with LaJuanita when he got to Augusta and moved in somewhere.

Requests like this, especially to a guy like Waymon's boss, excited the man no end. Waymon said slowly, with a canned hesitancy in his voice, "Well... I just don't... *know*. An extra ten minutes. That's a *lot*, you know. Ten minutes could alter the state of the future of TrustTrust Banks Incorporated—*Waymon*"

"If I'm back any later," Waymon said seriously, "you *dock* me."

"Oh, Waymon, I wouldn't *dock* you. But you know I *could*."

"*Dock* me."

Waymon made a sinister smile and tried to put his hand on Waymon's shoulder but Waymon juked his shoulder to the left so Waymon's hand missed. "So *tell* me," Waymon moaned, "what's so im*poooort*ant that you need an extra *ten* minutes as opposed to an extra *eleven* minutes?"

Waymon looked at him. He barely, barely squinted.

"Well, pardon *me* then… okay… but as a seasoned manager of human beings in the *work*place, I'm always just so *fasci*nated by this moment in the work day. I read *books* about it."

Waymon really squinted at Waymon this time.

Waymon cocked his head, inquisitively. "Say—you're not in any sort of *trouble* are you? I could *help*. Or, come to think of it, if you're out looking for another *job*, I'll need to know right this instant so I can *fire* you."

Waymon looked at his watch. "Personal business."

"Oh. *Personal* business."

"*Personal* business."

"Oh, oh-*kay*. Well, *Way*mon, did you know that that's a signal to me as a manager of human beings in the workplace that you're *up* to something, you know, cloaking your sneakiness in those famous words"—Waymon made quote signs—" '*personal business.*' See, if you had an appointment with a *brain* surgeon to have your *head* operated on, you'd have written me a memo with all the fascinating *details*. But you *don't* have an appointment with a brain surgeon, *do* you—to have your head operated on? Or do you really have an appointment for an afternoon sexy massage, *Way*mon? Know what I'm talking about? Guys like you who have to *paaaay* for pleasure at those ubiquitous Asian *jack* shacks along our most attractive Confederate Victory Parkway? Know what I mean? *Jack* shack? *Spank* shop? *Slap* shop? *Squirt* bucket? Where anonymous and illegally imported fast-talking Asian women lubricate your little troublemaker, then vigorously massage your little troublemaker."

"No. I *don't* have an appointment to have my troub—"

"Right. *Suuuuuure*. So *Way*mon—running out for an afternoon lubrication and jack and spank and slap and squirt bucket sexy *massaaaaage*?"

Never, ever, in Waymon's life had he encountered such a person as Waymon. Waymon considered witnessing some of the more important Primitive Baptist beliefs to Waymon right then and there in the bank branch but he was in a hurry. Waymon pursed his lips. "*No*, I said. *Personal* business." Now Waymon's face was turning red and he was starting to twitch. He said deliberately, "I… have… got… to… *go!*"

"So *okaaaaaaay*—like going to the dry cleaners or going out to have a wart *remooooooved?*"

"I clean my *own* garments."

"But *Waymon*, you wouldn't hack off your own wart, *would you?*"

Waymon gave Waymon a hard, hard look. "I would if I *had* to."

Mr. Rafsooliwicki

Believe it or not, Waymon walked into an empty apartment.

Believe it.

Again.

Seems that Mitch and Ken had their bitches come up with the bail money, and then Mitch and Ken went right back on over and cleaned out Waymon again. This time they got (stole) a rental truck from Ryder instead of a U-Haul and were now heading for Scottsdale, Arizona with Waymon's shit. Why they chose Scottsdale, Arizona no one really knows, not even the bitches, who were mad that Mitch and Ken didn't invite them to tag along. Scottsdale, Arizona, the bitches had heard, was a real nice place.

Anyhow, when Waymon stepped into his empty apartment he was already in a sort of frenzy, him being so nervous about calling up Augusta National Golf Club and asking for a job even though the recent omen was a big one. But then he immediately felt better because he knew that if Mitch or Ken had been back, or some other guys, and if they left the second bedroom alone again, then this omen business was really, really working in his favor and in just a minute he'd be the new guy in the accounting department at Augusta National Golf Club.

With a shaking hand, Waymon opened the door to the second bedroom.

Omen city.

Except the overhead light that shone on his model of the Augusta National Golf Club clubhouse had been turned off by Ken because he felt sorry for Waymon for having to steal all his shit again and even though he thought Waymon was a creepy motha-scratcher, he didn't want his light bill to get run up.

But this definitely did it.

Waymon now figured he could probably ask to be head pro since the omens were coming in such powerful waves, but he didn't know that much about selling overpriced pro shop golf socks.

Waymon took the portable phone (which they did not steal, another minor omen) off the kitchen wall and took it into the second bedroom and shut the door.

He turned on the little light that shines onto the clubhouse—which made him feel even more wonderful—then held the phone up in the air as if he were displaying a fish he just caught and made one circle in the room showing the contents of the room to the phone. Waymon wondered what assignments he might get. Calling up members whose accounts were past due? Helping members with their investments? He thought TrustTrust had some real good ideas he could bring to the job. Balancing their checkbooks or whatnot?

Waymon had the number memorized, of course. Actually, he had it programmed into his phone. If he, for any reason, had to call Augusta National Golf Club, then the call could be made with absolute precision and efficiency. He pressed the button and listened to the awesome beeping of the phone number of Augusta National Golf Club. He smiled. Waymon was now as calm as a sleeping infant, and wasn't at all surprised how quickly the phone was answered at Augusta National Golf Club.

Good things happened there.

Yes.

Lives changed for the better.

Of course they did.

Waymon Poodle knew this.

"*Good morning!* Augusta National *Golf* Club! This is Betty *Simp*son. How may I *help* you?" The voice was as sweet and as pleasant as Shirley Temple's. Well, why wouldn't it be? Waymon assumed that Augusta National Golf Club hired only the most congenial people in the world.

Waymon, still just as calm as a sleeping infant, just minutes away from getting the job even though he had to bother with the formality of asking for it, said, "Yes. Hello. I'm calling to inquire about working in your accounting department."

"Well isn't that *wonderful!*" Betty said "wonderful" as if she were competing in a contest for who could say the word with the most gut-wrenching exhilaration.

Waymon gazed at his golf clubs. He felt more wonderful as each second of his life passed. "Yes, *thank* you."

"No sir, thank *you* for calling Augusta National Golf Club. And *your* name?"

"Yes. This is Waymon *Poodle* calling."

"Mr. *Poodle*," she said as if hearing from someone thought to be dead for thirty years, "It's so good to *hear* from you!"

Obviously she was expecting my call, Waymon thought. But so cordial of her to go through these niceties.

"And you'd like to work in our accounting department?"

"Yes ma'am. I would. *Very* much. And as soon as possible."

"Then you just hold the line, Mr. Poodle. It will be my honor to connect you to the head of our accounting department, Mr. Emiglio Rafsooliwicki, who is in complete charge of hiring people for the accounting department and who is not on his phone right now and is sitting at his desk and is not at lunch either. As a matter of *fact*, Mr. Rafsooliwicki told me not *two* seconds ago that if anyone called for him, even if he didn't know the person or even if the person was a *sales*man, or even if he was about to lick a taco or take a bite of a clam sandwich or even if he was in a *meeting* or on the commode, to connect that person to him immediately and without hesitation."

"Thank you so much."

"May I connect you now, Mr. Poodle?"

"Yes, *please. Thank* you."

"My *pleasure* Mr. Poodle. I will connect you now to Mr. Emiglio Rafsooliwicki, the head of our accounting department. And thank *you* again for calling Augusta National *Golf* Club!"

Click.

"You're welcome," Waymon said to the hold music, which was the finest hold music he'd ever heard in his life, which he got to listen to for approximately sixteen minutes. No problem. No problem at all. The music was airy, uplifting, easy to listen to. Of course. It was the hold music of Augusta National Golf Club. I'll listen as long as you folks feel I need to, thought Waymon Poodle. Take me into your arms.

"WHAAAAAA!"

Waymon jumped.

"Emeeeglio Rafsoooliwicki on the phone here! Can I *hep* you now please—*yes?*"

Waymon instinctively felt he needed to raise his voice since he was all of a sudden talking to a foreign person. "Yes, this is Waymon Poodle calling to inquire about working in your accounting department."

"Whaaa! Don't talk to me so loud, Mr. Waymon Poodle!"

"Sorry."

"You want to work in accounting department did you say to me?"

"Yessir. I have a feeling there might be an immediate opening?" Waymon was pretty darn sure. Mitch and Ken. Two times.

"*Why* you want to work in accounting department, Waymon Poodle, when I have way too many crazy men-stroooo-a-teeng lunatics in my accounting department already!"

Waymon wasn't expecting that one. "Well, sir—"

"What do you do *now* Mr. Waymon Poodle calling to work in my accounting department?"

"I'm a *bank* teller."

"Whaaa! A bank teller! A bank teller isn't an accountant I don't think!"

"But I believe," Waymon said with a rising tone of panic, "that the *skills* of a bank teller are certainly, in this case, transfera—"

Just then someone screamed so loudly that Waymon could hear it in the background. Some horrible, screaming woman: "This Mr. Farnsworth wants a two-dollar-and-fifty-cent credit for a soda! He's the fourth richest man in the world!"

"You stop that screaming right now about that Mr. Farnsworth! I'll fix *him!*"

Still screaming: "You got his number?"

"Memorized!"

Waymon thought it sounded like a mental hospital, although he'd never been in a mental hospital. He'd only seen some on TV. "Uh, Mr. Rafsooliwicki?" Waymon said meekly.

"Yes, this is Emeeeglio Rafsoooliwicki! Who is this please talking to me? And did you know I was about to eat a clam sandwich!"

"Waymon Poodle. We were just discussing—"

"About how you want to work in my accounting department while I'm about to take a bite of my clam sandwich and call a member to tell him he can stick the two-dollar-and-fifty-cent credit for a can of soda up his hairy—?"

"Have I called at a bad time?"

"*No,* Mr. Waymon Poodle. Not at all. It's been a pleasure speaking with you today. Now I bite my clam sandwich."

Click.

Inhuman Resources

Betty—her real name was Betty, Betty Simpson—punched the inter-office number of Frank Johnson, otherwise known as Emiglio Rafsooliwicki, head of the accounting department at Augusta National Golf Club. As Frank Johnson was not about to bite a clam sandwich, he picked up his phone. "Yeah?"

"Whatcha think?"

"*Strange.*"

"How long you *do* him?"

"Sixteen minutes. He was still on the line when I picked up, humming along with the hold music. Stravinsky. Who in the fuck knows Stra*vin*sky music?"

"Damn."

"I know."

"Hey, *Frank.* Employees can't say 'fuck' in the clubhouse. You didn't get the memo?"

"I didn't get the memo. But *they* say 'fuck' all the time—the goddamn *members.*"

Betty gazed at the oil portrait of Jimmy Carter for a moment. She forgot to give Frank the memo. "Well, anyway, you give him that crazy men-stroooo-a-teeng lunatics bit?"

"Yeah. Nothing. Didn't seem phased at all."

"Did you do the thing about the members stealing range balls?"

"That's gotten old, actually. We did the Farnsworth soda credit shtick. I had my new girl scream it."

"*Wow.* This guy wants it bad."

"No kidding. You got him pulled up yet?"

"I will by the time you get up here."

"Coffee? Cold Red Bull?"

"Coffee. You know how I like it."

"Sure do—you nasty thang."

Computer whirring now. All Betty typed was "Waymon Poodle" into a special Interpol-Royal Canadian Mounted Police-Scotland Yard-CIA-

FBI-Justice Department program. That was it.

Frank put the mug of coffee down by her mouse. "Seems to be taking a little longer than usual."

"I know. There can't be many Waymon *Poodles* in the world."

"Betty, you've been doing this for *way* too long to think his goddamn name is actually—"

"Shut the hell up, Frank. Here he is."

"Wow," Frank mumbled. "His name really *is* Waymon Poodle and he really *is* a bank teller at a grocery store. Mullet Luv? Where the hell is Mullet Luv?"

"Northeast Georgia somewhere. I'll bet he's inbred."

"Well—pull up some pictures. That'll tell you right there."

Two simple keystrokes. Waymon's past and current driver's license pictures popped onto the screen along with three satellite pictures taken of him just last Tuesday loading groceries into his Chrysler Diplomat. "*Wow.* Looka *this* guy."

"Damn. Remind me never to spend the night in goddamn Mullet Luv."

"Frank, watch your *mouth*. Some dip wad member might walk in. I'm sure we can't say 'goddamn' either." Betty glanced through the window at the driveway in front of the clubhouse, then back at the screen.

Frank said, "Do voice evaluation."

"Yeah. Good idea." Betty called up the entire Poodle-Simpson-Rafsooliwicki conversation which had been recorded by the computer and evaluated by a software program designed by a number of eminent psychologists, psychiatrists, astrologers, and sociologists, as well as the CIA, the FBI, and some seasoned criminals. Betty hit the "Report" button, and then they leaned toward the screen. Betty said, "Well now. Says here he's extremely regional, honest, intelligent, loves the Masters, the golf course on which it's played, the wonderful sport of golf in general, and the iniquitous allure of what goes on behind the gates of ootsie-tootsie private golf clubs. Says he loves collecting golf memorabilia and golf magazines, lacks a few of the more sophisticated social skills but can still communicate with other human beings in his own particular way, and he's a hard and loyal worker. Oh, looka here. Guess what freaks him out?"

"His reflection?"

"*Funny*, Frank. Says here he's afraid of giant cicada killer wasps, as opposed to just *regular* wasps. Says regular wasps don't scare him one bit. Now ain't *that* strange."

"This creep's *all* strange, Betty."

"Now, on his dangerous side, just one characteristic—obsessive—but he's the type of person who will channel it for something he thinks is vital to life it*self.* That's it. The whole report. Dam*nation.* This is one focused *cat.*"

"The *hell* with this guy, Betty. He's pulling one on us so bad it's historic. I just feel it. Pull up the bio. Birth to today. This is the new software version, *right?*"

"Yeah. That smelly, butt-crack geek from the CIA installed it for me yesterday. God, I had to spray the room after he left. His hair had goddamn wasp nests in it."

"This is the one that includes bank accounts, physician records, credit card use, web site time, and magazine subscriptions? All that other shit?"

"Yeah. Oh… *look.*"

Betty and Frank leaned toward the monitor again, as if their heads were connected. Usually, birth-to-today bios on every person who calls, writes, plays as a guest, digs a hole under one of the fences and urinates on a green or goes skinny dipping in one of the ponds or pulls up a chunk of something, or is on the ticket list, every vendor, every other whacko or scum bag who drifts into the air space of the radar of Augusta National Golf Club is ten to twenty pages long.

Waymon's was half a page. Real boring stuff. Said he spent an hour an evening going back and forth through the Masters tournament web site. Never once—not once—pulled up a porn site. He'd never even checked a stock because he didn't own one. There was even a question on the screen, "Does the subject occasionally speak in Tongues?" followed by a box that the system checked or left blank. The box was checked.

"In all my years," Betty said with a sigh, easing back in her chair, "I ain't *never* seen a fucker like this. Says he's a virgin, too. That wouldn't be the case with you, Frank—now *would* it?" Betty lit a cigarette.

"Baby, I ain't been a virgin for a long, long time. Like since I was *nine.* Go back to his pictures."

Betty pulled up Waymon's pictures again.

Frank pointed at the screen. "Look. He's wearing the same tie in every shot. Kind of nerdy, don't you think?"

"Of course, Frank—you dumb ass. It's nerdy as all *get* out. I mean who, other than the goddamn *members*, wears ties with the club logo every single day. *Jeee-sus.*"

"I swear, Betty. We need to have this dude checked out. Let's send Dick up there to Mullet Luv and check his ass out."

"Waste of time. Where's Dick been for so long anyway?"

"Cincinnati. Went to make sure that old McFarley guy was really dead."

"So, take his dried-up ass off the ticket list after sixty-two years?"

"Oh, yeah. I forgot to tell you. Got Dick's e-mail this morning. McFarley is as dead as *shit*. Dick decided to have him exhumed and have his DNA tested, you know, to be sure it was McFarley. So honey, pull up McFarley of Cincinnati on the computer and hit de-*lete*." Frank smiled an evil smile. "Never used his tickets anyway. Never scalped, never gave them to a friend or relative. Just sat on them. Sixty-two goddamn *years*. What a piece of shit. Who do these patrons think they *are*?"

Betty pulled up the McFarley file. Hit delete. Took one millionth of a millionth of a second. *Blip!*

"So why not? Dick's *perfect* for the Poodle case."

"I'll tell you why not." Betty spun around in her chair and gave Frank a sexy look, then eased her hand between his legs and began rubbing, then squeezing, fairly hard, his scrotum. "Because I think this Poodle is actually a normal person. I got a good gut feel on this one. I mean, we don't spend seventy-eight million a year on all this software and investigative time and new satellite acquisitions on the invasion of the privacy and the strict adherence to Masters ticket policies of sixteen billion people for fun. *Right?*"

"*Yeah*, baby. Squeeze like you *mean* it."

"Frank, pay attention—the system ain't lied *yet*." Betty tapped the screen with one of her sharp red fingernails. "Says right *here*."

"Tonight I'm gonna spank you so bad your pink booty's gonna turn a purplish ma*roon* color."

"Oh… that's *reeeeal* sexy talk, Frank, *dumb* ass. Anyhow, my gut tells me this flaming squid's running down the usual list and the phone's going to ring in just a minute and it's going to be Waymon Poodle of Mullet Luv, Georgia calling now to see if he can become a volunteer for the tournament. Perfectly normal. He really was nice when you think about it. A corn cob butt-rubbing hick from Mullet Luv—but *nice*."

Frank was boning up pretty good. He said in a voice he was sure was sexy this time, but still sounded pretty clunky, "Baby, you a-*maaaaze* me with your uninhibited and spontaneous acts of foxy, physical love."

Betty appraised Frank for a long moment. "Well, *Frank*—you're getting more amazing by the *inch*, you greasy halitosis *sleaze* bag." Betty took a big drag from her cigarette and blew smoke in Frank's face.

Frank began to lean down anyway, with his tongue already poking two inches out of his mouth, to French kiss Betty, who was seventy-nine years old. Frank, forty-two. Just then the front door blew open and four-hundred-and-thirty-two-pound Herman Whorthawg, a member for fifty years of Augusta National Golf Club and the third richest human being in the world (self-made chicken parts rendering magnate from Cow, Texas) who just so happened to be the newly elected chairman of the Radar and Air Space Committee of the club and the long-time Tournament Volunteer Discipline Committee Chairman, rumbled toward the reception desk. Mr. Whorthawg had never once in his life been told that he bellowed when he spoke even though people always cringed and sort of leaned back when he spoke/bellowed at them.

Betty stopped squeezing Frank's scrotum and tossed her cigarette into Frank's coffee mug. "Mr. *Whorthawg*! Good to *see* you again! How was your submarine trip to the polar ice cap?"

"OVERRATED!"

"Well, I'm so sorry to *hear* that!"

"BETTY! CUT ALL PLEASANTRIES. HOW'S IT LOOKING OUT THERE TODAY? MY FELLOW MEMBERS CROWDING UP THE COURSE AS USUAL?"

Seven-and-a-half-hour rounds today. Waiting on every shot.

Betty lied, "You'll have it all to your-*self*!"

"STIMP?"

"Seventeen!"

"TOO SLOW! WHO DO YOU HAVE TO FIRE AROUND HERE TO GET THEIR ATTENTION? HAVE THEM SPEED UP THE GREENS BEFORE I GET OUT THERE!"

"*Yes*, Mr. Whorthawg! I'll find someone for you to fire."

Mr. Whorthawg glanced at Betty's computer screen, then openly gawked. "HOLY LORD IN HEAVEN HAVE MERCY SWEET PRECIOUS JESUS!" WHAT'S WRONG WITH THAT PERSON?"

Betty said as if she were describing someone who just died, "Mr. Whorthawg, this is the latest catch. A Waymon *Poodle* of Mullet Luv, Georgia, who just called."

"TRYING TO GET ON, HUH?"

"Afraid so. Yes."

Mr. Whorthawg wagged his big fat pointing finger, which also had a bellowing quality to it, at Betty then at Frank who sort of snapped to attention so quickly he jerked coffee all over his club-logoed tie. His purple penis was already at attention. "IF I EVER SEE THIS SPACE ALIEN-LOOKING PERSON AT AUGUSTA NATIONAL GOLF CLUB SO MUCH AS ROTO-ROOTERING AN EXPLODING COMMODE—"

"*Yes*, Mr. Whorthawg," Betty said.

"*Yes*, Mr. Whorthawg," Frank said.

"THEN YOU TWO WILL BE IMMEDIATELY AND WITHOUT HESITATION RELIEVED OF YOUR—"

"Yes, Mr. Whorthawg?"

"Yes, Mr. Whorthawg?"

Mr. Whorthawg lowered his voice just a little: "DO I NEED TO CONTINUE?"

"*No*, Mr. Whorthawg."

"*Yes*, Mr. Whorthawg."

"WHAT?"

Frank croaked, "I mean—*no*, Mr. Whorthawg."

"THAT'S WHAT I THOUGHT. NOW ALERT MY CADDIE!" Mr. Whorthawg started for the secret locker room door, bumping the one-hundred-and-ninety-eight-pound solid gold bust of Dwight Eisenhower off a side table and onto the floor. Fat finger pointing at the bust as it rocked back and forth: "SOMEBODY PICK THAT HEAD UP!" Then he disappeared through the door.

Betty gripped Frank's scrotum again.

Frank flicked his tongue at her.

Then they both said in unison: "What an *irk*some individual," and began rubbing their hands all over each other's bodies while they French kissed enthusiastically.

And the phone rang again at Augusta National Golf Club.

Volunteerism

"Good morning! Augusta National *Golf* Club! This is Betty *Simp*son. How may I *help* you?" Her voice was yet again as sweet and as pleasant as Shirley Temple's.

"Yes. This is Waymon Poodle calling again?"

"Mr. *Poodle*," she said as if hearing from someone thought to be dead for thirty years. "It is so good to *hear* from you again!" Then Betty breathed into the phone with a hand cupped to the side of her mouth as if discussing something confidential, "How did it go with Mr. Rafsooliwicki?"

"He seemed to be about to bite a clam sandwich."

"Well, Mr. Poodle, he is a busy *man*. Busy, busy, *busy*. Always about to bite a clam sandwich. Did you get the job?"

"I'm not sure."

"Would you like to speak with him again?"

"I'm not sure."

"Well, he's probably about to bite another clam sandwich anyway. Or sometimes he's about to lick a taco. You know, if the man's near a snapper, fresh or spoiled, he goes nuts for that, too, that Emiglio. Well, *any*how, is there something *else* I can do for you Mr. Poodle?" Betty said as she flipped open the safety cover of a bright red button on her desk, then poised her finger over the button of a device that could, depending on how she felt that day, mildly or severely electrocute the head of the person on the other end of the line.

"Well, yes, there *might* be."

"And what is that? How may I *help* you?"

Waymon swallowed hard. "I'd like to inquire—"

"*Yes*, Mr. Poodle?"

"—about how to be a volunteer for the tournament. You know, the—"

"The Masters?"

"Yes. The... *Masters*." Waymon took a huge breath.

"Well isn't that *wonderful*!" Betty said "wonderful" as if she were competing in a contest for who could say the word with the most gut-wrenching exhilaration. "Well, Mr. Poodle, you've certainly called at the right time and to the right place. This *is* the home of the Masters, and I am extremely pleased to announce that I have an *immediate* volunteer opening, even though the tournament is just one week away and even though we have such a huge and loyal volunteer corps that we haven't even *needed* a waiting list in the last twenty-eight years. It's truly unbe*leee*vable that we can accommodate your request at such incredibly short notice, but we're more than happy to. *More* than happy."

Betty fired up another cigarette. That chicken-lip-rendering piece of— threaten *me* with my job? After sitting my butt in this chair with no armrests for over half my life listening to you scream and complain for fifty years? Yes indeedie—I think I'm gonna stick a Poodle four feet up your rear end, Whorthawg. Betty took a suck of that cigarette as if it was the last suck she'd ever get.

Waymon's heart began to race even harder. He tried to speak, to say thank you one thousand times, Mrs. Simpson, but nothing would come out.

"Mr. Poodle? Are you *there?*"

Nothing.

"Are you *there*, Mr. Poodle?"

Finally, faintly: "Yes. Don't you need, uh, a resumé or anything? References? A personal meeting with the board of directors? Do you need to talk to the assistant pro at the Mullet Luv Golf Center about me?"

"Not at *all* Mr. Poodle. We actually know all we need to know," Betty said as she squinted at a satellite photo of Waymon talking to man who, *damn*, looked exactly like Rhett Butler. "And we are absolutely honored that you've picked Augusta National Golf Club and its rich and historic major tournament heritage and whatnot in which to lend your time and skills as opposed to some hideous Australasian golf event in Fiji or something."

"I think I'm about to *faint*, Mrs. Simpson."

"Then you just go right ahead and faint, Mr. Poodle. And when you wake up you can look forward to to*morrow* morning, the earliest and most ex*pensive* delivery, where one of those nice Federal Express truck drivers, hopefully wearing those tight little blue shorts, will deliver to you at the TrustTrust Bank branch in the Publix grocery store on Confederate Victory Parkway in Mullet Luv a package from me with *all* the details on how to be a Masters volunteer and how to get signed up for the volunteer outing in May where you'll get to play the Augusta National Golf Club course as well as our par *three* course. Actually, you'll have an entire *day* to play as much golf on the two Augusta National Golf Club courses as you can possibly pack in before the sun goes down. And it's all *free*. And now that you're in the volunteer corps, you're a volunteer for the rest of your *life* and can play golf at Augusta National Golf Club every single year for the rest of your life on volunteer day, you know, if it doesn't get rained *out*, but volunteer day hasn't been rained out in thirty-nine *years*. Just remember to bring your own golf balls and clubs. We don't have rentals, so we have to turn away a lot of Japanese guests. So how does *that* sound, Mr. Poodle?"

Nothing.

"Mr. Poodle?"

A Docking

The wound in the center of Waymon's forehead—obtained by fainting, then falling upon the cupola of the clubhouse model of Augusta National Golf Club in the second bedroom of apartment 1931—was hideous.

It was a wound that looked as if someone held Waymon down and reared back and clocked him one good time with a ball-peen hammer. The wound, bloody in the center, with a swollen purple and yellow ring around it, seemed to visibly throb, as if it had its own heartbeat. If Waymon had ever looked like an individual who'd popped in from outer space, he did now.

Waymon, the branch manager Waymon, was actually tapping his wristwatch when Waymon walked, or sort of stumbled, into the employee break room of the branch office. "This has *certainly* been a new and fascinating interpretation of an extra ten minutes, Mr. Poodle."

"Like I said, *dock* me."

"Oh I most certainly *will*, because since I'm the boss I *can!*" Waymon caught a look at the wound as Waymon brushed past him. "My *God!* What sort of personal business were you *up* to?

"The *personal* kind. Now I need to go serve my valued customers. Excuse me."

"*My* customers? It's *our* customers! They're not all *yours!* And not with that creepy bloody *mess* on your pumpkin head!" Waymon shouted at Waymon's back.

But Waymon was already at his window, squawking, with unconditional professional affection, for the next valued customer to come and be served.

Let's Get It ⊛n

A FedEx delivery guy, the next morning, in tight little blue shorts, rushed through the two sets of sliding doors at the Publix on Confederate Victory Parkway, took a left and approached Waymon as he sat at his window waiting for a valued customer.

But not a valued customer because it was Waymon Boner sitting there and not Waymon Poodle. Waymon Boner, even though he was a branch manager, secretly thought customers were a horrible nuisance and did not particularly value them. He was also upset that he had to work a window today because Katrina, a large woman teller who couldn't hear well and absolutely refused to shave her mustache and had a tattoo on her neck and who had just gotten off the boat from Latvia, had to leave for the day as she'd broken both her arms and legs that morning on aisle eight. She had slipped on a shrimp. A shrimp she had started to "sample," but had spit out on the floor. Then slipped on it. Waymon was also upset that this Latvian person who had only been working at the branch for four days, would probably "own" Publix after a couple of legal proceedings. So there he sat, Waymon, upset: angry at the way the world worked.

"Waymon?" the FedEx guy said, holding a letter-sized package.

"Yes?"

"Sign here. Thanks."

Waymon looked at the address block on the FedEx package. From Augusta National Golf Club. A Betty Simpson. Nice handwriting. To a Mr. Waymon R. Poodle. "*Ohhhh*," he moaned, looking over at Waymon next to him, serving Old Mrs. Willard again. "This is for Waymon *Pooooo*dle." Waymon motioned with a thumb over toward Waymon.

The FedEx guy hated it when he got held up by being sucked into some weird internal office joke or people who obviously hated each other or some funked up attitude. Plus, these Waymon guys looked real strange. The FedEx guy and Waymon Poodle did the signing tango and the FedEx guy rushed back out. Waymon, upon reading the address blocks, felt his forehead wound begin to pound again, his throat squeeze shut, and without thinking he handed Old Mrs. Willard, instead of her money, a yellow Post-

It pad and a stapler.

Waymon Boner, mouth open, watched Waymon slink toward the break room without asking permission. Immediately, on instinct, without hesitation, and even before Waymon got to the break room door, Waymon mashed a little buzzer button that buzzed in the break room. When the break room buzzer buzzed, it meant that help was immediately needed up front even if an employee of the branch were having a heart attack or eating a burrito. Waymon mashed the buzzer twice: *buzz… buzz.*

Waymon sat at the break room table, hands trembling with excitement, and opened the package. He pulled out its contents. Reverently, his mantra exited his mouth. "I'm gonner tee it up at Augusta National. They didn't touch the stuff in the second bedroom. Mitch and Ken didn't touch the stuff in the second bedroom."

Buzz… buzz.

On Augusta National Golf Club stationery, in memo form, written to Waymon from Betty Simpson, in crisp, boring, old-school, conservative, twelve-point New Times Roman, were the following words:

THE MEMO: Augusta National Golf Club is honored to have you as a volunteer for the Masters golf tournament. I personally know that your involvement will alter the future of Augusta National Golf Club.

WAYMON: "Dang."

Buzz… buzz.

THE MEMO: And your volunteer number will be 1931.

WAYMON: "Dang… *dang.*"

Buzz… buzz.

THE MEMO: This Sunday morning you are to meet, at exactly 9 o'clock, the Augusta National Golf Club Radar and Air Space and Tournament Volunteer Discipline Committee Chairman, Mr. Herman Whorthawg, in the amphitheater of the media center, to be briefed on your duties as Manager of the Rope at the Practice Facility Invitee Entrance and Exit and to pick up your volunteer credential and yellow helmet. Please be prompt. You will be the only volunteer to be briefed as you are the only new volunteer to be accepted into the group in twenty-eight years so Mr. Whorthawg is excited that he has something to do.

WAYMON: "I get a *helmet.*"

Buzz… buzz.

THE MEMO: When Mr. Whorthawg enters the room, please immediately stand up like you've been shocked by electricity and face Mr. Whorthawg directly and when he asks your name, please tell him your whole name slowly to make sure he understands your whole name one hundred percent and extend your right hand to see if he wants to shake it. If Mr. Whorthawg seems stunned and doesn't say anything for a moment and/or begins blubbering and huffing and puffing his cheeks or looking around the media amphitheater like he's trying to find somebody playing a joke on him, say your whole name again, a little more loudly the second time, and tell him you're the guy from Mullet Luv, Georgia. Waymon Poodle from Mullet Luv, Georgia. More than likely, he'll immediately exit the media center real fast and your meeting with Mr. Whorthawg will be concluded at that point. Just make sure you grab your volunteer credential and yellow helmet and appear at your post promptly at 8 o'clock Monday morning in real boring khaki pants, a real boring white golf shirt and clean sneakers. You get a smock from us.

Buzz... buzz... buzz.

WAYMON: "Okay, then."

THE MEMO: Directions to Augusta National Golf Club and its media center are enclosed. (They were enclosed.)

THE MEMO: Once again, we are pleased to have you as a volunteer. Your presence at this year's Masters will be, because of this feeling I have, not ordinary. Now please read the next correspondence. Thank you very much.

Buzz... buzz.

The next correspondence was a hand written letter on heavily perfumed pink stationery from Betty Simpson to Waymon. The next correspondence also included a helpful photograph at which Waymon was very focusly gazing.

WAYMON, very focusly gazing at the helpful photograph: "Oh, my *Lord.*"

Buzz... buzz... buzz... buzz

THE NEXT CORRESPONDENCE: Dear Waymon, On a personal note, you need a place to stay. I called all the motels and they're booked, as usual. North to Raleigh, south to Orlando, west to Phenix City and East to Myrtle Beach. So I've got a wonderful proposal. Why don't you stay with me? I've got a one bedroom apartment and you certainly won't sleep on the kitchen floor or in the bathtub so you'll just sleep in my bed on top of me.

Okay? Don't worry. I'll be happy to cook and take great care of a void in your life. I know you have a void. Know what I mean? Your particular void? Really, where else were you going to stay? In the trunk of your car?

Buzz… buzz… buzz.

So, come see me in the clubhouse after your meeting with Mr. Whorthawg Sunday morning and I'll go over the exciting details. Let's Get It On, Betty.

THE HELPFUL PHOTOGRAPH: Betty was sitting by a swimming pool with a cigarette in one hand and a can of Miller Lite in the other. Dark sunglasses. Dark tan. Big smile. Sharp yellow teeth. And a teeny weenie leopard-skin bikini.

Buzzzzzzzzzzzzz.

Give a Damn

That afternoon after work, Waymon was in the parking lot of Sans Souci fiddling with his trunk lid.

Closing it, but not hard enough for it to catch. Then pushing the lid back up again and poking his head in the trunk, looking around in there, then he'd pull his big head back out again then poke his big head back in again.

Mr. Gable was out walking his Chihuahua with one of those electronic leashes with the shock button and watched this odd scene for a moment from behind a pickup truck. Then, on purpose, because Mr. Gable was fairly bored, he and the Chihuahua snuck up behind Waymon and Mr. Gable hit the shock button and the Chihuahua barked real loud and it scared the shit out of Waymon. Plus, Waymon thought Chihuahuas were, of all the dogs in the dog world, messengers of some kind. He thought that for no good reason, really, that they were messengers of some kind, Chihuahuas, but had no proof. That's just what Waymon thought and God forbid Waymon Poodle change course on something.

Mr. Gable got a good chuckle seeing Waymon bump the back of his head against the sharp tab of the lock.

But of course Waymon had that irritating, Christian, unconditional, and immediate power of forgiveness, and even as he was in horrible pain and rubbing the back of his head and gazing at that Chihuahua, Waymon asked Mr. Gable how he was doing today.

"If I was any bettah," Mr. Gable said in his horrible, New York-infected, forced Charleston, South Carolina accent as he went to town on a piece of gum, "then I'd have to be locked *up*." Mr. Gable gave Waymon a strange look. "You know what I mean there, Waymon?"

"I'm not really sure what you mean, Mr. Gable. But I'd certainly hate to see you locked *up*."

"Well, what would you want to see me, you know, *do*?"

Waymon turned and poked his head back into the trunk. "To have a nice day."

"Hey, I can live wid dat."

The reason for all this innuendo, imbedded in every single conversation every single time Mr. Gable encountered Waymon in the years they'd lived at Sans Souci together, was that Mr. Gable secretly thought Waymon might be a hit man from any number of very, very upset New York, New Jersey, Detroit, Las Vegas, Los Angeles, Philadelphia, Miami, Chicago, Boston, Kansas City, Biloxi, Reno, Atlantic City, New Orleans, Toronto, London, Tokyo, Tunica, Hong Kong, and Moscow crime families. Mr. Gable asked, "Mind if I ask watcha doin' there, Waymon, lookin' around in ya trunk, there?"

Waymon was so focused on what he was doing he didn't say anything, so Mr. Gable shocked the Chihuahua again so he'd bark. The Chihuahua barked.

"Hey!"

"I asked whatcha *doin'* there."

"I'm trying to see if a person could fit in the *trunk* space."

"Like *who* are you thinking might need to fit in the trunk space there, God forbid?"

"Me."

"*You*, Waymon? And why would you need to fit into the trunk space there?" Mr. Gable, at this moment, was as sincere as he could be, as he was an expert at putting whole bodies and bodies that had been altered in order to fit into trunks of cars, and he sincerely felt he could, after all these years, really connect with Waymon and assist him with something useful, even if the body was still alive and squirming when it was placed into said trunk.

"I'm gonner need a place to stay while I'm on a special vacation next week."

"You tawkin about stayin' in da *trunk?*"

"Yessir."

"Sleepin' in da *trunk?*"

"Yessir." Waymon turned and gazed into the trunk of his Chrysler Diplomat and smiled. He spread his arms. "Yessir. Right here."

"Lemmeassyouaquession."

That Chihuahua barked again.

"Where would youse be goin' where you gotta stay in a stinkin' *trunk?* Unless ya fuckin' *dead.*"

Waymon reached out and patted the Chihuahua's head. "Augusta."

PART III

A Bermuda Grass Masters

As for Mr. Whorthawg

Herman Whorthawg was not having a good Masters week not one bit.

His particular anxieties began Sunday morning: the tournament week hadn't officially started yet, and there he was having to huff and puff his cheeks out and look around the media amphitheater like he was trying to find somebody playing a joke on him. Well, not having to. To him it came naturally, the huffing and puffing part, sure, but it took a lot of energy to do it at that rate.

Folks just didn't understand. It also took a lot of energy to be the third richest human being on earth and the newly elected chairman of the Augusta National Golf Club Radar and Air Space Committee and the long-time Tournament Volunteer Discipline Committee Chairman and to deal with the hurricane force of this Waymon Poodle of Mullet Luv situation. Plus, he was already overwhelmed with the volume of mail being sent by some crazy woman to Masters invitee Chi Chi Rodriguez which, in the former role, he had to collect, read, and then go off somewhere and figure out what to do about. And this wasn't the usual amount sent to the Puerto Rican professional in advance of the tournament, one letter and a post card or a fax. But this year, whoever this woman was, had sent Mr. Rodriguez eight hundred and forty-eight hand-written letters on stinky pink stationery. So Whorthawg had opened the first one, then another, and all the others. Some time during the Masters, she was planning to show Chi Chi her _____ because she couldn't get as worked up when she thought about showing her _____ to Hale Irwin or Loren Roberts.

My God, Whorthawg thought upon each reading of a letter. Written by hand, no less, the obscene word. Fine, you sex freak woman, but why not show it to Mr. Rodriguez at an event in Palm Springs or Las Vegas? This is the Masters, ma'am. The goddamn *Masters*.

So see you at the Masters, each note warned at the end.

Whorthawg had never seen such depravity in his life. Why would some woman want to show Chi Chi her _____?

Plus—*plus*, this was the first time in his life someone had not done what Herman Whorthawg told them to do. The source of his additional and extreme displeasure was right there in front of him, not ten inches away. Waymon Poodle of Mullet Luv, Georgia, who had said his whole name real slow and where he was from, just like Betty Simpson told him to. Waymon Poodle, who was supposed to have been not allowed onto the property. Not even to fix an exploding commode.

And now he was one of my volunteers?

Whorthawg was blubbering and huffing and puffing. Nothing understandable was coming out.

Waymon was sort of reaching for his yellow helmet and credential held by Whorthawg's personal Pinkerton who seemed nervous too.

Then Whorthawg, as Betty Simpson predicted, immediately left the media center real fast.

Waymon stood at attention for another ten minutes or so just to make sure. To make sure of what he didn't really know.

Mr. Whorthawg, on the other hand, charged up to the clubhouse and banged through the front door to find Betty Simpson with a finger poised over the "Enter" key of her keyboard. Kind of in a hook-like position.

"BETTY!"

"Hi *Herm*. What's shakin'?"

"I JUST THOUGHT YOU'D LIKE TO KNOW THAT WAYMON POODLE IS ON THE PREMISES."

"You're not *pleased?*"

Whorthawg suddenly sensed something, as he was a sensitive person. He squinted at her computer monitor, then at her finger crooked over an important key, then back at the photo of him fornicating with President Clinton on a nice blue and white striped Martha Stewart lounge chair on the sun deck of a nice yacht by a nice side table with two uneaten shrimp cocktails. But not the two of them fornicating with other people as couples who may or may not be swinging. Simply, Herman Whorthawg fornicating with the President. "IS THAT ME THERE, WITH A MARIJUANA CIGARETTE BETWEEN MY LIPS, ON TOP OF THE PRESIDENT OF THE UNITED STATES, FORNI—?"

Betty leaned toward the screen for a closer look. She tapped the screen with a sharp fingernail. "That's you, *yes*, right there, making monkey love to Hillary... a *lot*." She moved the monitor so he could see the picture better. "See, I've got this great new software program where I can cut and paste photographs together and extort folks such as yourself. Well, not a bunch of folks. Just *you*. Of course, I have some recent satellite shots of you and your downstairs maid doing the afternoon delight on your diving board back at the ranch. Those shots are real, although I can't tell who's flinging around the riding crop. I love your expression. Like to see those, too?"

Whorthawg grabbed his chest, then his neck, and then his chest again. "QUESTION!"

"Yes?"

"AND WHY DO YOU HAVE YOUR FINGER POISED OVER THAT KEY THERE?"

"Well, *Herm*. If I happened to press this key *here*"—Betty barely touched it with the tip of her sharp looking fingernail—"then this photograph, and its brief paragraph of descriptive information that I wrote myself, describing who the two people are in this photograph having flagrante de-lec-*ta*-to and smoking and inhaling the smoke from a marijuana cigarette, would be sent by an e-mail blast to your board of directors, your shareholders, and your fellow members. And, oh, to all the golf writers in the world who would be extremely interested in knowing more. And there are a lot of golf writers. You're a *right* wing Republican, right?"

Whorthawg grabbed his chest, then his neck, then his chest again, then leaned toward Betty, then cleared his throat, and dramatically adjusted his tone. "What would, Betty dear, say, keep you from, say, pushing, Betty dear, that button there."

"Well, first, two million dollars."

"I'll write you a check immediately. Pocket change. *Glad* to do it. Certainly."

"Second…"

"Second?"

"Second, and finally, since all this computer programming has about worn me slap out, why don't we allow our friend Waymon Poodle to have a wonderful Masters volunteer experience. And let's just make sure he's first on the list to play on volunteer day next month. I think it'll make his *life*. Sound okay?"

Whorthawg grabbed his chest, then his neck, then his chest, and then his checkbook and wrote Betty Simpson a check for two million dollars.

"I forgot. And one other thing. *Sorry*."

Whorthawg gave her a pretty mean look.

Betty pushed her finger in the direction of the key that would change the rest of Herman Whorthawg's life schedule.

Whorthawg made a pleasant expression. "And what would the *other* thing be? How may I assist you?"

"During the tournament, Waymon will need someone to bring him his lunch every day and an afternoon snack with an iced tea. Waymon loves iced tea, sweet, with, pay attention: nine freakin' lemons. Not *seven* lemons or *ten* lemons. *Nine.* I also performed some additional research on our boy and believe it or not, he actually loves our pimento cheese sandwiches and a new computer program I just bought from the CIA and the Culinary Institute of America predicts that he's going to eat, in four point six seconds for each consumption, between two to three hundred of the things this week with*out* breaking a world record for mammalian diarrhea production. So Herm, *honey*, have a waiter in *mind?*"

So Herm was not yet having a good Masters week not one bit.

Nakajima Sez

As for Waymon, Masters week was going real super great.

For Waymon, in a word, *intoxicating*. He kept repeating it to himself, this lilting word, just under his breath, with his chin up. The Masters and the golf course on which it is played is… int*oxi*cating. Thank you Jesus for this intox – i – *cation* because now I stand here on the hallowed grounds of where men golf.

And thank you Jesus for this view of the clubhouse and behind me the sounds of eager patrons sitting in the Augusta sunshine in these green bleachers. Their conversations on golf, their favorite invitee. Thank you for that. Thank you for allowing me to overhear an informed, sophisticated, cerebral, attentive patron saying to his friend, "See, Edmond, the way the back of Jose Maria Olazabal's left hand is perpendicular to the target line at the moment of impact? *See?*"

And the man's friend had said, and Waymon had been intoxicated hearing his incredible and observant and awe-inspiring response, "*Yes*, Samuel. I *did* see that our Spanish friend and two-time Masters champion's left hand *is* perpendicular to the target line at the moment of impact, and even right *after* impact for a moment. Yes, I *saw* it! That's such an important thing to *do* in golf."

"*But*," Samuel said, "I've *also* read, Edmund, where you don't want your left hand to be perpendicular after impact for *too* long, as it's urged by some of the finer teaching professionals that a golfer turn his hands over soon *after* impact."

"Samuel, you *certainly* must realize, my fellow lover of golf, that so *much* of what we're told and so *much* of what we read about the mechanics of the golf swing *is*, well, to be *frank*, contradictory."

Tiger Woods, Fuzzy Zoeller, Tommy Aaron, Roberto DeVicenzo and their caddies all backed up at the rope there, wondering when this dumbass, inbred, wall-eyed hick is gonna open his eyes and lift up the goddamn rope and let us through so we can go warm the fuck up.

"Contradictory, *sure*. But *per*haps, Edmond, that's what makes the game of golf so incredibly wonderful, mysterious, and forever challenging on a supremely personal basis."

Waymon, nearly weeping. Floating toward heaven.

"Samuel?"

"Yes, Edmond?"

"Praise Jesus for *golf*."

"Edmond?"

"Yes, Samuel?"

"Jesus *made* golf."

Oh, thank *you* Jesus, Waymon pondered with his eyes clenched shut. Praise you for golf, for bringing golf into our lives, for saving our *lives* with golf. And thank *you* for this incredible yellow helmet, which fits perfectly and that I think I can keep.

Intoxicating.

And why not?

As Manager of the Rope at the Practice Facility Invitee Entrance and Exit, Waymon Poodle stood in an action spot, a spot where important action took place. A spot made for the most decisive and poised volunteer. Here comes Seve Ballesteros out of the clubhouse. Seve Ballesteros coming this way with a wad of autograph seekers tripping over themselves, agitating him. Shoving things at him. A couple of Pinkertons. His caddie, with the heavy golf bag on his shoulder, muscling forward. Keeping it moving. So when to pull the rope aside for such great men and their caddies? Sometimes the great man and his caddie and his swing coach? Sometimes the great man and his caddie and his swing coach and his agent and his golf psychologist and his nutritionist? When they're ten feet away? Five feet? Twenty feet and risk some kid squirting onto the practice range to grab something and run off and hawk it out there on Washington Road?

Certainly not. Most certainly not.

Waymon Poodle of Mullet Luv, Georgia determined that the pulling aside of the rope, begun with a confident pulling up of the end of the rope which had been tied into a loop, from the end of a beautiful green metal rod thrust into the ground by some obvious expert, some expert who had gone around the entire grounds of Augusta National Golf Club thrusting beautiful green metal rods into this sacred soil at the most exact and logical places—that the decision to pull the rope up and off the rod and to move aside with the rope in one hand and to gently, but with a certain amount of authority, sweep back these beloved patrons with the other hand, was made on a case-by-case basis. And Waymon Poodle was in charge of making that case-by-case-basis decision from 8 o'clock each morning until the final invitee left the practice range. Charles Coody, six feet. Funk, nine. Goosen, Hjertstedt, Struver, and Gogol. Hennie Otto, Bruce Fleisher, just depended. And so on.

And so on they came. Still wearing metal spikes most of these great men, their clicking on the asphalt, a warning. Here I come. I'm serious about this. Move outta the way folks. I appreciate your affection for me and that you want me to sign something and smile at you and touch your kid on the top of the head or give you a golf ball or my lucky Krugerrand but I'm comin' through. Got to warm up, find my swing for today. I wanna win the Masters real bad, a shit load more than those *other* three major championships of the year and I'm not going to the British Open this year because I hate the weird, unpredictable weather—well, you can predict it: it sucks out my greasy butt every day—and I hate the courses they choose and the gross food and those drunk little dried up caddies they got over there that they force on you, so I got only one of three major champion-ship chances this year. I do, folks. Really wanna win the Masters. Look at the expression on my face. Looking serious. Real serious and focused on hitting it close to the pin and making a shit wad of putts, especially saving the big ones for TV on Sunday. Came all the way from Sweden, came all the way from South Africa, came all the way from Arkansas, came all the way from England, came all the way from the toilet in the men's locker room to win the Masters, so get the hell outta my way and I'll pat your kid on the head later and give him my golf ball after I walk off eighteen after shooting something real nice in the low sixties. Thank you so much. Now let me go win the Masters.

Tommy Nakajima, on Monday, spikes clicking, had said something to Waymon in Japanese as the rope was lifted by Waymon. "Look at this guy who might be from outer space limits." And Waymon knew it was a com-pliment. Surely it was. The great Japanese professional. Yes, say it slowly. *Nahhh – kahhh – jeeeee – maaaahhhh.*

Waymon bows to him now, every morning, upon his coming and going.

Sluman, Palmer, Jack Nicklaus. Mize, Parnevik, Eichelberger. Their paths crossed each day in this holy place. Waymon Poodle, wide eyed. Rich Beem. Esteban Toledo. Sergio Garcia's dad.

Kids wanted Waymon's autograph, too. But I'm not an invitee, Waymon protested. But felt flattered. *You* again. Didn't I give you my autograph yesterday? Waymon chuckling, but still signing the visor, the cap, the hat, the occasional sweaty bicep. Now I told you yesterday I'm not an invitee. I'm not *any*body. I'm just Waymon Poodle, Manager of the Rope at the Practice Facility Invitee Entrance and Exit. I'm just so... so *happy* about all this. I just... can't wait... to play Augusta National Golf Club next month, all day until the sun goes down, and for the rest of my life on each and every volunteer day, including the par three course. No, kid, I'm not crying. Well, I can't *lie* to you, I guess it's all this... intoxicating, beautiful pollen.

Q & A With Huge Pecker

Most promptly, at noon on Wednesday of Masters week, Leonard "Huge Pecker" Leboeuf, chairman of Augusta National Golf Club and the Masters, strode into the media center amphitheater with his green-jacketed mob of one hundred or so committee chairmen waddling behind him for the annual golf writer welcome and briefing.

Noon was real early in the morning for golf writers.

The only other time in their lives that they're awake and doing something at that ungodly time of day, is if they're teeing off at some real nice private club, or exceptionally real nice public club, or exceptionally real nice resort, after goofing the head pro or the general manager or vice president of marketing for a free round of golf. Otherwise, there they are, golf writers, sitting in the Augusta National Golf Club media center at noon on the Wednesday of Masters week for the annual golf writer welcome and briefing from the chairman, really wanting to be drinking coffee and smoking a cigarette in their hotel room in their underwear wondering why they're aren't any real good titty clubs in Augusta they can go enjoy after a hard day of golf journalism.

The real and unspoken incentive for a golf writer to be sitting on his or her ass and acting real quiet at noon in the amphitheater of the Augusta National Golf Club media center on Wednesday of Masters week was that if you didn't show up for this thing then your chances of being chosen out of the golf writers' lottery to play Augusta National Golf Club all you want the Monday after the final round of the tournament for free was swirled down the toilet.

The golf writers who were awake, since nothing else real big was going on in the world of golf at that moment, were wondering why the new chairman of the club, a man of such stature in the world of industry and commerce and golf, went by the nickname of "Huge Pecker." Seemed like "Big Pecker" would have done the job. Plus, they were still recovering from the last chairman's nickname: "Felix." And the chairman before Felix insisted he be called by the world of golf, "Hootie," whose real name was Butch or something like that. So there they were, golf writers, from all over the world, wondering about these important things in all their different languages.

Huge Pecker, seated behind the podium, clearing his throat a lot, waited for all the committee chairmen to get settled in along the walls of the media center. This took a little while as some committee chairmen were over one hundred and ten years old and were facing the wrong way or were muttering something about being up at such an ungodly hour and wondering why there still weren't any real good titty clubs in Augusta. Twenty-eight committee chairmen had nurses trying to hold them up.

The media center was finally real quiet as all the golf writers were afraid to breathe or make their chairs squeak or have their cell phone go off or their laptop computer batteries go dead and make that beeping noise as this would also, they were pretty sure, be a mark against them in that lottery business.

"Boys," Huge Pecker said real smooth into the microphone in a Cajun-type drawl. He was an oil tycoon from Louisiana. Twenty-four handicap. Big slicer. Former L.S.U. fullback. Was dating Elizabeth Taylor and was afraid he might have gotten her pregnant last week. "We welcome you to Augusta National Golf Club and wish you good golf typing. Each year at this time I read a wildly informative, prepared statement to you boys and then look forward to your questions. As you *know*, I am happy to answer any questions specifically pertaining to the toonamint and the golf course. Even questions about the goddamn *driving* range are okay with me. Go crazy. But questions concerning anything about the club and *us* guys are strictly forbidden, and if you *ask* me one then that'll be a mark against you concerning the media day *lottery* business. We keep a big list of shit around here, as you *know*. So if any of you boys ask me one about the club or us guys, then sometime this week I'll sneak up behind you while you're typing something—even if some of you women are *men*—and fuck you *up*."

All the golf writers shifted uncomfortably in their seats and looked around at each other. One golf writer's seat squeaked a little bit and he almost passed out.

"*So*, the first order of business is to tell you that we have the first new volunteer in twenty-eight years. His name is Waymon Poodle and he's from Mullet Luv, Georgia and also resides in Mullet Luv and he'll be efficiently lifting up the rope to the invitee entrance and exit at the practice facility and then efficiently putting the rope back down on the metal rod all week, you know, when an invitee wants to go warm up or whatever. I also hear that this gentleman is real funky looking. Anybody give a shit about this Waymon Poodle?"

In unison, one hundred or so golf writers murmured, "No, sir, Huge Pecker!" And one hundred or so shrugged their shoulders. Snaps. Pops. One guy thought he had broken his spine, but he bit his right pointing finger, almost in two, to keep from screaming.

"Fine, *fine*," Huge Pecker said. "Furthermore, Augusta National Golf Club wants to acknowledge that we know that *you* know that some *crazy* woman has been sending the club letters about how she is planning to show Masters' invitee Chi Chi Rodreeeguez of Pota Reeco a certain part of her *person* during this year's Masters. *How* you have obtained this information is most amazing to me as we really try to keep this sort of thing real quiet around here and Herman Whorthawg behind me, Chairman of the Augusta National Golf Club Radar and Air Space Committee and Toonamint Volunteer Discipline Committee Chairman, is quite at a loss as well, as he told me he locked up all the crazy woman's letters in his locker and hid a few behind some socks in the *pro* shop. Why *anybody* would buy overpriced pro shop golf socks is a mystery to me when there's a nice Dillard's right out there on goddamn Washington *Road*. Nonetheless, we know that some of these letters have been obtained by you folks and that you've been reading them in your underwear and passing them back and forth to each other in the bars in your hotels and giggling. We know that *you* know that in this crazy woman's correspondence that she has used the ob-*scene* word regarding the particular part of her body she plans to reveal to Mr. Rodreeeguez. Certainly, boys, you must do *your* job, but we must do *ours*. In your reporting, Augusta National Golf Club asks you, instead of using the ob-*scene* word, to use the following words." Huge Pecker paused for a moment, whereat hundreds of golf writer breaths could be heard sucking in, in anticipation.

A lady golf writer from Tennessee thought the words might be, "Her Priscilla Presley."

A golf writer from England thought the words might be, "Her Naughty Bit." Then he thought about it a moment longer, and then changed his mind to, "Her Very Quivering and Mysterious Naughty Bit."

A golf writer for a newspaper in Alaska thought the words might be, "Eskimo Fever," as he was intensely fantasizing, at that very moment, about some Eskimos who lived in the apartment above him back home.

A golf writer from Charlotte, North Carolina thought the words might be, "Her Quail Hollow."

Sitting in the front row, a lady golf writer for *USA Today*, who was pretty darn sure it was Huge Pecker who had some goons sneak into her office and change around her typewriter keys after she wrote that column that exposed to the world that Augusta National Golf Club didn't have any members who didn't have peckers, didn't care one bit about what words he wanted them to use. She lit a long fireplace-style match, leaned over onto her left butt cheek, lifted her right knee way up then moved it way over to the right, put the end of the lit match very close to her anus, grit her teeth, groaned, growled, turned red, then turned purple, and cut an astonishing fart she'd been saving for three and a half weeks—since the tournament at Doral. The blue fart flame was eight feet long.

Huge Pecker ducked behind the podium, into which she carved her initials with the tip of the flame, which was hissing. Huge Pecker thought about getting one of his Pinkertons to haul her out by her hair, but then he figured that if she had the ability to produce a blue fart flame, especially an eight-foot-long blue fart flame, then he didn't want to tangle with this kitty. He had a goddamn golf tournament to run. So Huge Pecker decided to have some flowers, golf socks, and a case of pimento cheese sandwiches sent over to her hotel room. Huge Pecker popped back up real quick and raised a finger in an important looking way.

The golf writers quit thinking about what the words might be and crushed out their cigarettes and cigars and dumped the contents of the bowls of their pipes on the floor and gave Huge Pecker their absolute and supreme attention. Even that lady golf writer made her fart flame stop. When the flame flew back into her anus it made a backfire *pop!*

Huge Pecker said, "'Bermuda grass,' *boys*, if you please, in the place of the ob-*scene* word. These precious words, 'Bermuda grass,' which are well known to those who love and respect the game of golf, were chosen by me and the men you see standing behind me in a big super-special meeting late last night over highballs and crudités. The words are spelled capital b-e-r-m..."

All the golf writers sucked in a real deep breath and started scribbling, spastically, on their note pads or typing, spastically, on their laptop computers as if they were being told in advance the numbers for the Super

Lotto.

"… u-d-a g-r-a-s-s. Bermuda grass should be capitalized, say, if the usage is in a headline such as, 'Bermuda Grass Watch Continues at Augusta National Golf Club,' you know, it being the first word in the sentence, but you probably know that kind of thing by now." Huge Pecker cleared his throat as he looked around the amphitheater to see if any golf writer looked offended. They were all smiling brightly at him. "Okay. Furthermore, Bermuda grass should be used as a noun in most cases. If you use Bermuda grass as a *verb*, as in 'Mr. Rodriguez got Bermuda grassed over by a pine cone on Flowering Crab Apple during the second round,' then that would be, well, correct, I *guess*. Anyhow, Bermuda grass, boys. Thus endeth my prepared remarks. Welcome once again, by God, to Augusta National Golf Club and the goddamn *Masters*. Let's get her done."

Since playing in the media day outing was so important to the quality of their lives, and the two percent discount they got in the Masters merchandise mart, the golf writers stood and gave Huge Pecker a rousing applause that might have lasted for four or five years until Huge Pecker raised a finger again and they all shut up and sat down real quick.

"Thank you. I will now entertain your questions concerning this year's toonamint."

An arm raised: the hand at the end of the arm wiggling and flapping and twisting and squirming and thrashing around as if the hand were competing in a goodbye waving contest. Front row. Gary McCord of CBS in a lime green polyester jacket and an Augusta National Golf Club logoed tie and white, starched, button-down shirt and gray pants with a fabric belt with Augusta National Golf Club logos all around it and shiny oxblood Weejuns with Augusta National Golf Club-logoed ball markers in each one where pennies would go and his hair absolutely perfect and some cologne, but not too much. His eyes weren't puffy and it smelled like he'd brushed his teeth and finally shaved the greasy handlebar mustache off and everything. Actually, he had the mustache in a plastic bag in his pocket for good luck.

"*Please*," Huge Pecker said in a real sophisticated way.

Gary stood up and asked in perfect vocal modulations, "Huge Pecker, how much does it cost to get in?"

As if on cue, everybody laughed and laughed and slapped each other on the back and laughed and chuckled and pointed at Gary. This question he'd asked every year for the last seventeen years was sort of meant to be an ice breaker, but Gary deep down really, really, really wanted to be a member of Augusta National Golf Club and he thought it was a good way to secretly but openly learn as he was, like a lot of folks who join expensive golf clubs, thinking about cashing in his poorly performing golf stocks to cover the initiation and the first few months of dues and pro shop purchases.

But, oh, no.

Huge Pecker was chuckling too, but in a Cajun accent-type way. "Well, now, *Gary.* You know I can't answer *that* question. How are the chill-ren?"

"Doing *great* Huge Pecker. Hey, you know the best part about kids, Huge Pecker?"

"What's that, Gary?"

"*Makin'* 'em."

Huge Pecker laughed so hard he gagged. "And how's Mrs. McCord doing? She's a pretty *gal.*"

"I'll tell her so. I surely will tell her, Huge Pecker. Sure will."

"Fine, *fine,*" Huge Pecker said, then turned around to see if any of his committee chairmen were paying attention.

One was. The chairman of the Tee Marker Placement Committee.

"Now, *Gary,*" Huge Pecker said, "you talk good on the TV this weekend, okay?"

"Oh, I *will* Huge Pecker. I'll mention the fine job you're doing—a fuckin' *lot.*"

"Fine, Gary. *Fine.* How are you hittin' it lately?"

"I shot a seventy-*six* the other day. I did. With a darn *quad.*"

"Super, Gary. Just super, a seventy-six. Other questions, Gary?"

"Speaking of *gals,* Huge Pecker."

"Yes, *gals…*"

"Do you think you and your ubiquitous bucket-hat-wearin', red-nosed, potbellied, palsied, cirrhotic, corporate CEO, hush-mouthed, Irish, good ol' boy, smug-as-shit, hog-jowled, over-par, bald-headed *members* will ever let some ol' saddlebag-butt, slow-playin', quadruple-bogey-makin', vodka-slurpin', constantly-complainin', cigarette-suckin', mustache-wearin', corporate C-E-O, over-par, *fat* woman be a member in this incredibly wonderful golf club?"

"Fine question, Gary. *Fine.* Only under a most com-*pelling* circumstance."

"Huge Pecker, please *give* us"—Gary waved his arms four or five times in dramatic, circular motions as if he were showing someone the Atlantic Ocean—"an example."

"Well, Gary, all I can say at this point is… that I'll *know* it when I *see* it."

"The compelling circumstance?"

Huge Pecker raised an eyebrow. "Yes, most certainly. I'll *know* it when I *see* it. Just like I just *said.*" Then he rolled his eyes and made a face.

"Okay then," Gary said. "Would this be the compelling circumstance, you huge question avoider?" Gary made a gesture with his hands as if he were measuring the size of a woman's breasts. Then he made another gesture as if he were holding the breasts up and weighing them, then another gesture, specifically with his fingers, as if he were squeezing the breasts, then twisting the nipples with the tips of his thumb and pointing finger.

Huge Pecker tilted his head appraisingly, then rubbed his chin.

Then, Gary stuck his tongue out as far as it would go, then flipped his tongue up and back in his mouth and then did the whole tongue thing sequence about three or four more times.

Huge Pecker raised his other eyebrow. Then lit another cigarette.

Gary then put both hands behind his head, interlocked his fingers, and pumped his hips as if he were fornicating. He was also making a loud snarling sound. And then Gary pushed his tongue hard onto the inside of his mouth over and over and made a certain hand gesture, universally agreed to be the imitated act of oral sex. Then Gary sat down and winked at Huge Pecker two good times. Gary scribbled a note to that lady golf writer for *USA Today* which asked, "Can you teach me how to do that? Like, during lunch?"

Huge Pecker winked back, just once. "Now, Gary," he said, "don't lecture to *me!*" then laughed so loudly the microphone shorted out and blew up, then was replaced less than half a second later by an Augusta National Golf Club audio-visual expert escorted by a Pinkerton. Huge Pecker said, "Other incredible questions from our golf writers?"

A hand raised. Sort of in the middle right. Glare off the diamond pinky ring was real bright.

"*Please.*"

Rod Suntan of the Las Vegas *Lost Wages*, who, in a secret ballot by all the golf writers in America, was voted to be the horniest golf writer on planet earth and was acclaimed for always having some humid sexual angle in every golf story he wrote, even stories about Craig Stadler or an agate score. "Rod *Sun*tan, babe, of the Las Vegas *Lost Wages?*"

"Please. What is your question?"

He was smacking gum. Really going to town on it.

"What is your *question?*"

"Say, Huge Pecker babe, where and *when* do you think this ol' gal will show Cheech her Bermuda grass?" Smack, smack. Pen ready.

"Rod, we don't exactly know. As is our policy, we'll let you folks know as soon as *we* do, so you fellas can be right there on the spot to observe the Augusta National Golf Club Bermuda grass situation and type a word or two about it for your various publications."

"Hey thanks." Gum smacking. Gave Huge Pecker a wink and pointed at him. "Nice jackets."

"*Thank* you."

Hand raised. Sort of in the middle left.

"Domo," Huge Pecker said.

Domo? What the *hell?* Isn't that Japanese? The golf writers turned to look. Huge Pecker knows Japanese? Oh yeah, that crazy little guy every year.

It was that smiling Hajime "Jimmy" Yamazaki of some hard to pronounce, much less read, newspaper over there, so they never voted him anything. They could have voted him friendly, though. He was real friendly, and he smiled all the time like the dickens. And they could have voted him to have the distinction, without embarrassment, of wearing the same polyester plaid jacket with a striped shirt every day to the tournament. Like the dickens. They could have done that.

Jimmy bowed. "Ah, Huge *Pecker*-san. Bermuda grass o mite, shigoto ni ikitai *desu.*" Jimmy bowed again.

Huge Pecker pointed at him and smiled. "Hey, *Jim*bo. Tetsudatte kudasaimasen *ka?*" Huge Pecker asked, then laughed in Japanese.

Jimmy started laughing too. Just bent over laughing in Japanese.

All the golf writers looked at each other, then at Jimmy, then at Huge Pecker, and sort of shrugged their shoulders. Damn. What the hell was *that?*

Hand raised. Sort of in the upper middle.

"Domo—I mean please," Huge Pecker said, still sort of chuckling in Japanese.

Milt Limp of the New Jersey *Oppressor*, who, in a secret ballot by all the golf writers in America, was voted to be the nerdiest golf writer on planet earth and who hadn't, they were absolutely fucking sure, clipped his nose hairs or ear hairs or toe nails or changed his hairstyle or his glasses or his one golf shirt or his old brown leather belt with the double holes all the way around it or his horrid nasal voice since he began coming to the Masters in 1971. And he had body odor and showed around pictures of his kids who were weird looking. Although he'd won six Pulitzer Prizes for investigative golf journalism, so that was something. "Milt Limp, sir, of the New Jersey *Oppressor*?"

"Fine, *fine*."

"Huge Pecker, *sir*? That little maple tree way up in the woods on the eighth hole of the par three course?"

"*Yes*, Milt."

"I went out there early this morning and masturba—I mean, measured it with my hand-held global positioning system device for the third year in a row to see if you guys moved it during the summer? Three inches?"

"*No*, Milt. We moved it exactly, as a matter of fact, three inches and a quarter."

"Oh." Milt spastically scribbled something on his note pad then shook his little global positioning system device by his ear. "Huge Pecker, sir?"

"Yes, *please*."

"Why have you guys changed the pH level in the water in the pond at the sixteenth green? I went out there this morning and measured the pH level in the pond and compared it to my findings from the last twenty-four years? Does that affect the ball flight over the water? The pH level? Are you guys trying to affect the ball flight of the invitees over the water by adjusting the pH level of the water in the pond at sixteen?"

"*No*, Milt. Thirty-two Canada geese and a local mallard duck we know pretty well dropped in there the other day and conducted some fairly rude business. A new fellow on our maintenance staff named Toby is taking care of that today. Oh, and the pH level of the water in the pond at the sixteenth green *does* affect the ball flight by the way, so a real good observation there." Huge Pecker winked and pointed at him. "By the way, Milt, if you don't mind every day this summer when you fly around in that helicopter and take pictures of our course maintenance and construction activities, try not to fly so *low*. The rotors chewed up quite a few of our dogwood trees and some of our extremely rare azaleas last year. Okay? We did get the nice check from your newspaper, however."

"Well, Huge Pecker, what about a hot *air* balloon? Can I use a hot air balloon to see what you guys are up to?"

"Well, *Milt*, I can't *stop* you until we buy the air space above the course, which is a project for next year. Okay then, other ques—"

"Uh, one more question? Huge Pecker, sir?"

"Fine, fine, Milt. *Fine.*"

"Uh, Huge Pecker, how much does it cost to get in?"

In this case you spell dead awful silence with a capital "D-A-S."

Squished Cheese

A funny thing happened at the Masters.

Not "funny" as in "Haw! Haw!" funny, but funny as in unexpected: Herman Whorthawg fell in love with Waymon Poodle. But not "fell in love" as in Whorthawg and Waymon all of a sudden fell into dreamy homosexual male love during the first men's major professional golf tournament of the year, but "fell in love" as in Whorthawg gained a real affection for the new volunteer from Mullet Luv. It just took him a while.

Whorthawg, audibly grumbling on Monday as he made his way down toward Waymon at his post, held the pimiento cheese sandwich a little firmly—deliberately—before he gave it to his volunteer. Whorthawg had never brought a volunteer his or her lunch before. He'd never brought anybody their lunch before so there he was, audibly grumbling. He shoved it at Waymon. "Here's your *food*," he said huffily, then started to turn around.

But before he could storm off, Waymon said with extreme sincerity but with a tentative hand on the big man's green-jacketed elbow, "Mr. Whorthawg, I wanted you to know that it's an honor to be one of your volunteers. I deeply appreciate this opportunity to serve you, the Masters, and the invitees. Have a wonderful week."

Whorthawg stopped, turned, gave Waymon an odd look, and then clomped off. But then thought about it. Exactly what he would have said if her were Waymon Poodle at that moment. And sort of what he had said to his fellow members when he got elected to his chairmanships. An honor. To serve. I deeply appreciate it. But Waymon Poodle? An honor? What's so goddamn honorable about standing in the hot sun all day for seven days in a row with a yellow helmet on your head and doing it for free and gulping down those god-forsaken pimiento cheese sandwiches? We'll see if he feels honorable by Sunday afternoon. Whorthawg forced a fairly nice smile at Betty as he passed by her in front of the clubhouse.

And here she came, Betty Simpson, every afternoon, taking a cigarette break and making sure Waymon's lunch got delivered, but more so to see if she could cajole Waymon into coming over to her place that night. Virgin men were so rare, such a unique opportunity that she couldn't make herself sit still. Days in a row of it. The squirming. Frantic bedroom fantasies of her and Waymon getting it on like wild monkeys or bush hogs. Him bringing her coffee in the morning and lighting her cigarettes in his mouth and giving her one. His giant, country sausage accidentally flopping out of the purple satin bathrobe she bought him. Her grabbing it and pulling him toward her and then having hog sex. Or when Waymon wasn't looking, her just lightly sticking the end of her cigarette on the tip of it. Or her grabbing it and dipping the tip of it into her hot coffee. She had to have relief. She eased up to him.

"Sunday, you know, I waited all morning for you to come by," she said out of the side of her mouth. "I skipped church just fer you. Hurts to be rejected day after day, especially when there's love in yer heart. I bought a whole bunch of groceries, too, and a sexy purple satin bathrobe—for me *and* you. Matching."

Waymon really didn't know what to say, except: Well, thank you ma'am, uh, Miss Simpson, but he had a place. He was staying in the Diplomat.

The Diplomat? Ain't heard of that one. *New?*

Waymon sort of ignored Betty until she finally walked off. The type of heebie-jeebies she was giving Waymon every day gave him erections. And for Waymon it felt downright sacrilegious to have an erection at the Masters.

A Bermuda Grass Masters

Every morning after Waymon climbed out of his trunk in the parking lot of the Washington Road Waffle House, after he had shaved with an electric razor in the gasoline-smelling darkness and wiped off his nude body with a couple of baby wipes (aloe), he bought the local Augusta newspaper and read it with his breakfast.

"BERMUDA GRASS WATCH BEGINS AT AUGUSTA NATIONAL," the Thursday headline had blared. Waymon read the story, wide-eyed. He read every Bermuda grass story every morning, wide-eyed.

On Friday morning, wide-eyed, and no sign of the Bermuda grass yet, thus the headline read: "BERMUDA GRASS WATCH CALMLY CONTINUES AT AUGUSTA NATIONAL."

Waffle House waitresses are an astute bunch, customer-keen, newspaper readers, too. Pouring coffee, Waymon's waitress, the one he'd had all week, asked him what he'd do if that woman showed her Bermuda grass to him instead of Chi Chi Rodriguez. She had Waymon pegged as the kind of fellow who'd definitely grab some Bermuda grass.

"In my position of authority I'd immediately alert a Pinkerton and have the pre-verted woman removed from the premises," Waymon said to her, matter-of-factly.

She made a face. "You would, huh?"

"That's what I'd do. Alert a Pinkerton. Have her remo—"

"*Bull* shit. You wouldn't lean over and look at it, or grab the goddamn thang with your hand and let out a rebel *yell?*"

Waymon shoved a strip of bacon in his mouth. "Nope. Not *me*. You must be thinking of someone else. Some *fornicator*."

"*Huh*. So how are the hash browns? You gotta be *sick* of them by now."

"They're absolutely delicious."

So the delicious routine continued for Waymon Poodle, and for Herman Whorthawg. Waymon had a natural knack for getting attention. He finally got Whorthawg's, totally. Waymon knew more about the Masters than he did. He knew more about golf than he did, but the lunchtime talk was not provided to impress. Just to make a friend. A golf friend.

It took a few days of Waymon's weird charm, and finally Whorthawg knew he'd been wrong to judge this book by its cover. But the wrapper was just so strange. On Saturday, he confided to Waymon, just inches from his ear. "*Waymon*, this Bermuda grass–Chi Chi Rodriguez state of affairs situation, comes under my jurisdiction as Chairman of the Augusta National Golf Club Radar and Air Space Committee—"

Waymon lifted the rope for Tommy Nakajima and his caddie again. "Yessir."

"—so I've gone to every volunteer on the whole goddamn golf course (he lost twenty-one pounds doing it) and I've promised them a little two hundred thousand dollar gratuity if they can in any way spot the Bermuda grass situation before it happens and help us and the rest of the world avoid having to see this woman's Bermuda grass here at our beloved Augusta National Golf Club."

"Yessir." Rope up for Lee Trevino.

"All the magazines and newspapers in the free world and a large number of Communist nations are sending extra photographers, although this has become an extra ten billion dollar benefit to Augusta and the metro area. But I could lose my membership over this, Waymon, especially if this woman's Bermuda grass is particularly hideo—"

Waymon held up a hand. "Yessir."

"So it looks like I can *count* on you, Waymon? You're my best man. I know that now, by the expert and efficient way you take that rope hook off the metal rod and put it back on there. Just incredible."

"I'll be on alert, sir. I'll do what*ever* is necessary."

Whorthawg looked at the way Waymon's eyes pointed in different directions and knew he had an advantage over everyone else. He whacked Waymon's sweaty back and hustled off.

As for Chi Chi, why a woman wanted to show him her Bermuda grass at the Masters wasn't a problem one bit, he told Whorthawg and his member deputies in his Puerto Rican accent. Chi Chi was slurping up a bowl of grits.

They had asked him to attempt to feel as comfortable as possible this week as it wasn't like somebody was trying to shoot him like they were Hubert Green a while back in the U.S. Open or whatever. It was just some Bermuda grass a woman wanted to show him.

"*Well*, gentlemen," Chi Chi said in his Puerto Rican accent again, "I've been shot at. Theees is better. Seeing her naked beauty will help me *win*."

Whorthawg and his deputies stepped back for a moment and huddled. Have we ever had a Puerto Rican champion before?

No, by God, we don't think so.

What if he starts chattering in Puerto Rican at the awards ceremony and nobody understands him?

What kind of crazy spicy shit will he serve at the Champions Dinner next year? What if everybody gets the *squirts*? We don't want another fuckin' Vijay Singh eyeball dish!

They had to worry: Chi Chi became the oldest invitee ever to make the cut in the Masters.

The Sunday morning headline: "CHI CHI SAYS IN HIS PUERTO RICAN ACCENT TO BRING ON THE BERMUDA GRASS. SHOOTS THIRD ROUND LOVE NUMBER AND DEDICATES LOVE NUMBER TO THE MYSTERY WOMAN."

He was in the last twosome on Sunday with Tommy Nakajima.

The Sunday morning sub headline: "NAKAJIMA SAYS SHOW IT TO HIM INSTEAD. SHOOTS 69 TOO."

This was not the Masters they wanted.

And neither did Waymon. On Sunday, ever the traditionalist, and the supreme optimist, Waymon wanted to lift the rope for the final twosome he hoped would consist of Jack Nicklaus and Arnold Palmer, that the woman might have the decency to show Mr. Rodriguez her Bermuda grass over at the par three course by a stump or something.

Betty Simpson worked her way through the sweating wad of photographers and golf writers staked out at the invitee entrance and exit to the practice facility on Sunday. She was wearing a dress for the first time that week. "Whorthawg bring you your pimiento cheese today?"

"Yes, Betty," Waymon said distantly. He was watching in two directions, naturally. He made the mistake of calling LaJuanita about the two hundred thousand dollar Bermuda grass reward. He knew LaJuanita would go out and spend it.

It was hot. So very hot. And no breeze.

The Sunday sub-sub-headline: " 'IT'S GOTTA BE TODAY, DARLIN,' CHI CHI SAYS."

Waymon, so sad the experience was nearly over. The week so wonderful. The Wednesday night Bible study with forty-eight Masters invitees at the Holiday Inn Buccaneer Room. That, too. Incredible. Amazing they allowed him in. And allowed him to speak in tongues for a couple of minutes.

Whorthawg there now. Using his bulk and the power of his enormous green jacket to bump patrons out of the way to get beside Waymon who was still scanning the universe for the Bermuda grass. Whorthawg giving Betty a sour look. Hoping she'll enjoy that nice two million.

She would. She was going to go spend a large chunk of it right after she showed Chi Chi her Bermuda grass, as passionately promised Augusta National Golf Club in some recent correspondence, her Bermuda grass, hers, hers for you to see, Chi Chi, in slow motion.

And there he was, the victim, the Puerto Rican golf professional, coming at them through an open swath of patrons, Pinkertons holding them back with fat and skinny arms, the tournament leader doing his saber thing with his driver even before he hit his first warm-up shot, he was that fired up about this thing, Bermuda grass, winning the Masters, his hair as black as the bottom of Mariana's Trench, skin so brown and shiny, the metal spikes of his golf shoes three inches long, glistening so brightly, even through the building clamor you could hear them crunching on the boiling asphalt, Nakajima right behind him, looking over Chi Chi's shoulder through those thick, goofy glasses from the seventies, or has anyone told the Japs to look at a few of our fashion magazines to see they're way behind in the eye wear department, Nakajima, knowing that if he got in the Bermuda grass photograph something like this could mean big yen.

Betty lifting up the flowered dress with her bird-like claws to show Chi Chi Rodriguez her Bermuda grass on Masters Sunday. A Lillian Vernon dress, very nice on her as she was one of those genetically thin people, no one between her and Chi Chi so Chi Chi was going to get the full benefit, Chi Chi three strokes ahead of Nakajima on a Masters Sunday.

A lot of yelling and pointing now that the Bermuda grass was being revealed, the clicking buzz of one thousand Nikons and Canons and a whole bunch of Revco and Eckerd and CVS and K-Mart and Wal-Mart and Walgreen's disposables, a million patrons snuck in with them, a few thousand people with their cell phone cameras held up, scanning for it, the Bermuda grass in the sun now, tan lines dramatic, the cigarette still in her mouth.

She loved Chi Chi Rodriguez, why does everyone need to know why

she wants to show him her Bermuda grass? It's *how* that's the most interesting, it's how that gets shown on TV. Betty Simpson, sure, had completely lost it and was smiling anyway or was smiling because she had lost
it, anyway, really hard to say at this point which one came first in this most
public of psychosexual scenarios at a major golf event for men, but seemed
to have happened a long time ago, the losing of it, she had the fingernail
on the button of Technology, an employee with too much free time and
power, a thousand reasons why this sort of crazy thing happens at nice
golf clubs like Augusta National but no one with the time to explore the
reasons now, not now, no, not now of course, hey, safe to say at this point
that Betty Simpson really was the most powerful person in golf and *not* ol'
Huge Pecker.

Anyway, it's Masters Sunday, no time to explore and debate that now,
nope, a golf fan in Nebraska watching this scene unfold but also thinking,
why not just play the back nine only on Sundays at the ol' Masters and get
it over with so it wouldn't bump into "60 Minutes"? but knew it was un-
likely that they'd ever do it, you know, those hard-headed rich members of
that place, you know, just playing the back nine holes for the final round
and that's it, a big golf fan in Nebraska thinking that, Omaha, Nebraska.

Betty had adjusted the satellite to burn rolls and rolls of film over this
thing, well, of course she knew it was computer chip space, not "rolls" as
in the typical rolls of film like you get at Walgreens, called the satellite
over from monitoring some multi-billionaire fat cat vacationing at that
moment in Cabo Del Sol, wolfing down a platter of fish heads and watching the Masters, who had last Tuesday shoplifted nine pairs of socks from
the pro shop when he was a guest and now had it pointed at herself, Betty
did, pointed at herself, and the CBS camera right there, right on it, too,
herself, Betty Simpson and her exquisite and feral Bermuda grass, sexy,
sexy grandmaw type she was, gave responsible, middle-aged men and paw
paw types, too, and Methodist bishops who normally used good sexual
judgment, well, she made these men conjure up frantic sex fantasies about
her, Betty did.

On CBS, long-timer Verne Lundquist with the call but decided not
to say anything at first, you goof this one up and all of a sudden you're
Jim Nantz, banished, banished from the Monday after the Masters media
day golf outing for being so articulate and precise and appropriately senti-
mental at just the right moments on TV during the Masters, so he got the

heave-ho from Huge Pecker and his posse, he can't play for free, in other words, like we can, Lundquist was snickering, but the CBS director was screaming real loud at Lundquist in his ear plug to say something, this kind of thing was in your contract, you know, and you're obligated to make an intelligent comment when a woman shows everybody her Bermuda grass on worldwide TV during the fuckin' Masters, *Ver*-no baby, just remember, in calling historical moments in sports, less is *more*, less is more, so cough something up like that simple and spectacular contraction you barked in nineteen eighty-six when Jack baby rolled in the big birdie on seventeen, the big Yess-*sir*! I mean, *hell*, no one's going to hear what you say anyway, the director says, so Verne Lundquist, he's thinking, what the hell, here's one for golf and television and psychosocial and psychosexual history on the Central Broadcasting System: "Folks, what the whole world's been waiting for. There it is, you're looking *right at it*, the Bermuda grass. Yes *maaaa'am!*"

And perhaps planet earth shook for a moment as several, several hundred million viewers in all nations of the world went nuts all at once, seemed like planet earth did shake for a moment, or vibrate, really, as Verne Lundquist finally made the story of some woman, determined to show Chi Chi Rodriguez her Bermuda grass at the Masters, official, him being an important representative of CBS, and CBS being the long-time television network of the Masters and all.

Waymon's hand over the Bermuda grass first, dress pulled up to her neck now so you could even see her bra, a fairly typical black one but no one in the entire world was looking at the bra, they were staring at the Bermuda grass. Waymon now cupping the Bermuda grass with his right hand, warm, of course, good and hairy, of course, like a Brillo pad the Bermuda grass was, and moist. Hot in Augusta, Georgia in April sometimes, so Bermuda grasses get moist, but it's also been cool during a number of past Masters, but it was hot during this one, particularly today, the final round, so the Bermuda grass was moist, only natural that it gets that way when it's hot at the Masters, moist.

The middle finger of Waymon's hand all of a sudden sort of sinking through the Bermuda grass and into the other part—my God! Oh, my God! OH, MY GOD!—that's what Waymon was thinking when his finger did that, sinking through the Bermuda grass and into the other part, and now Waymon's also worried that his yellow helmet might fall off then he would be out of uniform and Waymon believed in the rules, then Whorthawg's hand over Waymon's, Whorthawg's expression one of utter seriousness even with all the sweat burning his eyeballs and the hot sun in his eyes and the flashes of the million cameras, of course his expression was one of utter seriousness, he was a serious man, he had to be in this broken, undisciplined world.

Waymon's expression, on the other hand, as if he saw a ghost, but looking right into the camera of the photographer of *Golf*, his favorite magazine behind the *Masters Journal*, but all of Waymon's golf magazine shooters were burning rolls, getting the money shot, the big cover shot, historic, absolutely golden portfolio material, hey, they could use twenty pages and show the Bermuda grass presentation in whole sequence form beginning when she was just an anonymous face in the crowd smoking a cigarette, like a swing sequence of Lee Trevino or Nancy Lopez.

Betty's expression now like a boozed up sorority party girl, clenching that cigarette between her yellow teeth, sort of a snarling expression, well, not sort of at all, it was a snarling expression, no doubt about it one bit.

Circus sounds, lots of them, circus sounds back up in Mullet Luv at the hair place where LaJuanita works, open on Sundays from noon to nine at night and LaJuanita and her hair dresser colleagues screaming, then gawking, then screaming, then gawking at the television up there in the corner, pointing at the television with their brushes in their hands, combs, scissors, blow dryers, jugs of gel. These gals and their customers knew nothing about golf, knew nothing about how golf was a multi-billion dollar industry and how imperative the Masters tournament held at Augusta National Golf Club was to the world of golf, knew nothing about how reverent and respectful things were supposed to be down there at the Masters, but knew for fucking sure that that was LaJuanita's fiancé there on television, in his yellow helmet, Waymon, the bank teller, the "sex monk" LaJuanita told her friends she had nicknamed him, with his hand on that old woman's Bermuda grass, and LaJuanita had already told her colleagues that Waymon's performance there at that golf tournament helping people or something like that as a volunteer helper or something helping people, well, girlfriends, they were gonner give Waymon two hundred thousand dollars as some sort of performance bonus which Waymon said she could have so she boogied on down to Atlanta last night with Karl, y'all know my old fiancé Karl, and bought a whole bunch of nice shit at the Rooms to Go for her and Waymon's trailer for when they got married and her and Karl stayed over at the Ritz-Carlton, her and Karl, she had the filet mignon and Karl had the chicken and then they ordered up one of them sex movies in their room, well, *three* sex movies for twenty-five dollars each, so thanks for everybody understanding why she got in a little late today and was limping a little.

Chi Chi saying in his Puerto Rican accent while he whipped a sixty-eight inch long driver around like a sword or saber or something like that while staring a hole in that Bermuda grass and then pointing the grip of the driver right at it, and saying in that accent of his, real loudly, "Hey, *doll*! Loo-keen *good*!"

So with that pronouncement, it's like starting a pit bull fight or cock fight or bar fight or WWF SmackDown thing as Chi Chi pretty much acknowledged that the Bermuda grass situation was now in full force and he'd had his look at it and now the rest of the world could have at it while he went and warmed the fuck up because here he all of a sudden had a chance to win the biggest cracker golf tournament there ever was and ever will be, him being a shiny Puerto Rican, too, yeah, boycott *this* boys, and Whorthawg—

Whorthawg liked it when things were in control, and now he finally knew he should have been more cordial to Betty, never in fifty years a kind word said to her now that he thought about it, even when she told everybody who'd listen at the club about how her Chihuahua got in her dryer and she didn't know it when she pushed the "On" button and it sort of dried up pretty thoroughly after forty-five minutes, she thought it was her cross training sneakers in there thumping around as she sipped her coffee and enjoyed a cigarette at the kitchen table while she read her *People* magazine, she moped and moaned about it for days hoping the members might understand that lonely old single women like Chihuahuas as pets, the Chihuahua's name was "Prissy," the help, Whorthawg thinking, deeply pondering them at this point, but quickly pondering them since he was busy, the little people, pondering them, they can do big bad things, don't give them time to think, and had also heard and read that super-sex freaks have shrieking orgasms doing this sort of thing: in public, no less.

HOLY LORD IN HEAVEN HAVE MERCY SWEET PRECIOUS JESUS! he bellowed like a moose when Betty finally cut loose on one, her pelvis was really, really juking around, and now Whorthawg knew with absolute certainty that super-sex freaks have shrieking orgasms doing this sort of super-sex freak thing on a boiling hot Masters Sunday on CBS.

And so did Waymon, the moist.

Rain Delay

Near Siloam, even though he remained, a month and a half after the event, one of the most famous or infamous people in the world, depending on your personal psychosocial or psychosexual predilections and understanding of what happened and why it happened during the final day of the Masters right there at the invitee entrance and exit to the practice facility at Augusta National Golf Club, Waymon hydroplaned and spun his Diplomat in wild circles from the far right lane of the eastbound Georgia Interstate 20—and right after, Waymon passed the "STAY OFF MEDIAN" sign and spun onto the flooded median for a few more wild circles then back into the eastbound direction of Georgia Interstate 20 without even stopping, like in a movie. So there he was, Waymon, just spinning on down the highway, but moving toward Augusta nonetheless. It's finally volunteer day at Augusta National Golf Club and Waymon is extremely excited.

He wasn't surprised he was spinning his car down the highway as the weather reports he was following on his crusty AM radio reported that the band of heavy showers moving down I-20 was the biggest band of heavy showers to hit the area since weather history was recorded. But boy, the radio announcer was saying, it sure is nice to finally get some rain. Sure is, after all that dry weather we've had lately... well, all last *year* when you really *think* about it, those poor *crops*...

The spinning of his car reminded Waymon, as he tried to man-handle the spinning steering wheel with his skinny arms, of the time those six giant cicada killer wasps all of a sudden appeared in his rear view mirror, then floated over the front seat and onto his face. Of course, Waymon knew that if he had left them alone and stopped the car and rolled down his window they might have flown out, but he had felt the need to swat at them and that was what really started the whole mess. Dang, he thought, and the one that kept clinging to the back of his hand with that pulsating yellow and black thorax.

His Christian psychologist had urged him not to daydream about giant cicada killer wasps. She had urged him, with a hug, but there Waymon was, daydreaming about them as he passed through Siloam... Camak, into Augusta, onto Washington Road, still raining so hard, so violently pelting his Diplomat, that Waymon took an early, incorrect, right turn off Washington Road and was immediately shocked to find that the Augusta National Golf Club guard house had been taken away and all those magnolia trees had been dug up and Magnolia Lane had been widened and a horrible double yellow stripe had been painted down the middle of the street. And now there was a barbershop on the right? They'd put homes on the practice range, with boats and motorcycles parked in the driveways, rotting Big Wheels in the uncut grass, barking dogs, rusting grills?

He was on Berckmans Road and didn't know it.

Raining that hard.

"Dang," Waymon muttered as he clutched the steering wheel with both hands. "*Dang.*" He could see police lights flashing up ahead, then two police cars pulled up to a monstrous thirty foot high mound of mud, caked dirt, and green grass on top of it all. White pipes poked from the huge pile at odd, broken angles, the mess was blocking the entire road. To his right, a sign blasted by shotgun fire, read "Rae's Creek." Waymon lurched forward and through the rain could see, like a single candle on top of a cake, a yellow flag. A golf flag.

It was the twelfth green of Augusta National Golf Club.

A policeman walked over to Waymon's window.

Waymon rolled the window down. "Wow, it's really raining hard, huh?"

"Sir, yes it is raining hard. Would you mind turning around? The road's blocked."

"Yessir. But is that a—?"

"A green. A *golf* green."

"A green from—?"

"Yep. Every year this son of a bitch gets washed down Rae's Creek. We report it. They come get it."

"Wow."

The policemen looked Waymon over and glanced into the back seat at Waymon's golf clubs. "Say, pal—you were planning to play Augusta National today?" The policeman laughed so hard he started choking.

Waymon, not yet crying, but still hopeful, pulled back onto Washington Road and saw a sign directing him to one of the gravel parking lots.

"Volunteer Parking." Waymon entered the lot slowly, reverently, and discovered that it was empty. Of course then he thought that when it quits raining he might have the whole course to himself, and even if he had to skip the twelfth hole then he'd just figure up what he thought he might have shot on it—probably a birdie—and that would be okay. Waymon pulled up to the far fence. Still raining so hard, the sheets of rain so white... yards away was Tea Olive... the green would be right up there to the right. He was squinting, looking through the passenger window to try and see it... but was jolted by a sharp knock on his window. Someone in a heavy yellow rain slicker with the hood pulled down. Spinning his flashlight around, signaling Waymon to roll down his window. Waymon rolled it down.

"You gotta be freakin' kidding!"

"Kidding about *what?*"

"You a volunteer?" the guy asked.

"Yeah. What do you think? Passing over pretty soon?" Waymon shoved his head out of the window and gawked up at the sky. Hard rain pellets hit him in the eyes.

"Passing over?" The guy cut loose a stream of tobacco juice across the top of the car. "Lemme show you something. Looka here." He pulled from inside his yellow slicker a device the size of a laptop computer. It had a screen. The logo on the top of it said "NASA."

Waymon looked at the screen. It was a portable Augusta National Golf Club maintenance staff issue weather radar device worth one hundred and forty-eight thousand dollars. Every maintenance employee had one. There were a lot of maintenance employees.

"You see this big ol' blob of red and purple?"

"Yeah?"

"And you know that blobs of red and purple is the *worst* kind of rain you can fuckin' have? As opposed to blobs of *green?* And green sometimes ain't even hittin' the *ground*. But you know stupid rednecks will sit there and look at that green color on the radar screen on the goddamn local news then run out of their trailers and look up at the sky and point and go, 'Well that don't make *any* sense, honey. The radar on the TV says it's raining on our house but it ain't raining on our house one *bit*. Not one fuckin' *bit*.'"

Attempting to be cordial, Waymon said, "Those crazy people."

The radar was spinning around real fast.

"So," the guy said, "You know what's underneath that big ol' blob of red and purple?"

"Augusta National Golf Club?"

"Augusta National *Golf* Club." The guy shoved the radar device back into his slicker and spit on the tire. He looked at Waymon without saying anything.

Waymon started to feel a little uncomfortable. It was a look Snort and Billy gave him right before they said something real mean. "So I don't guess we're—"

"Hey, boy! You're that crazy volunteer what grabbed Betty Simpson's Bermuda grass!"

"I'm afraid so."

"You know, I *thought* it was you… hoooo-*weee*! That musta been *hideous*!"

Waymon huffed like a three-year-old, then yanked it into reverse and drove back down to the twelfth green on Berckmans Road and lurched out of his car, knowing this was what robbing a TrustTrust branch feels like. From the other side of the window. Once you get the urge to do it, it's just real hard to stop. All that adrenaline and free money. All the voices in your head telling you this was okay—the teller probably won't mind if you don't point a gun at him and if the letter is well written.

Waymon marched right by the policeman who was trying to light a cigarette in the downpour— "Hey, you!" —and with both hands, viscously digging in with his fingernails and hands and skinny arms, scooped out a massive chunk of the green of Golden Bell. As Waymon knew a little bit about turf agronomy from some of his magazines, he made sure to get a lot of the putting surface and a lot of the roots.

He sped back to Mullet Luv from there, two hundred and forty-eight miles, to the Mullet Luv Home Depot and bought a plant light and went directly to the second bedroom, and shut the door behind him.

e-Pulsation

That night, late, dark and quiet, and because Waymon felt guilty about stealing some of Augusta National Golf Club, he felt he should punish himself some more even though he felt, at that moment, he was already living in an apartment 1931 waking nightmare.

Waymon crept into the second bedroom, turned his computer on, pulled up the Internet, and typed in that certain address given to him by his Christian psychologist, then hit Search.

Shakily, wearily, and with extreme tension, Waymon was hoping to ease his giant cicada killer wasp fears once and for all and thought that visiting this web site would make him feel better.

PROFESSOR JEEVPIL BISWAPATI'S ULTIMATE!
AND EXCLUSIVE!
GIANT CICADA KILLER WASP WEB SITE

http://www.georgiainstituteoftechnology.edu/Entomology/~biswapati/KILLER.html

May 2007

I am a calm and reasonable man. You know me as calm and reasonable. Because I am. I am calm and reasonable. But I must confess my excitement about the recent and painful death of my giant cicada killer wasp nemesis, Professor Lamar Feckle of the University of Georgia.

You, as loyal devotees of my lifelong work and research of giant cicada killer wasps, know how Feckle constantly disputed my findings and made fun of me on entomology talk radio shows. So I wear this thing on my head. It's called a particular kind of hat, by the way, not a towel. Fine. I am a Hindu and speak Hindi. So I have a long beard, which is braided and comes to a sharp point. And some fairly long fingernails that come to sharp points also.

Fine. I think I'm a pretty freaking hip dude.

He makes fun of me no more, that dead Feckle. I poke his carcass with a sharp stick. Now I have the only web site devoted to my beloved giant cicada killer wasps. Thus, Ultimate! and Exclusive! I goddamn use marketing-type words now. I am not a circus barker. I am Jeevpil Biswapati, entomologist. This is what Feckle has done to me.

But even though he was my nemesis and I was his nemesis I was still asked to observe the "crime" scene, if you will, because I am known as a smart dude, too. Crime? Yes. As I had long suspected, that dumb redneck was not satisfied that giant cicada killer wasps were big enough. Upon viewing his laboratory (I had to step over his dried up carcass; his eyes were wide open and they seemed to follow me around the laboratory like Mona Lisa), I discovered that Feckle had perverted Nature and had produced a gob of monstrous giant cicada killer wasps. Monstrous? Yes. Seven inches long my devotees, with some nasty "tude." Think of a common blackbird with a pulsating yellow and black thorax. Some he already had floating in formaldehyde just like in "Aliens" (see photo below courtesy of Warner Bros).

In his journal Feckle had named these beasts "super whopper" (*Superus* *whopper*us *hideous*). Thus, super whopper giant cicada killer wasps. Clunky, with a capital "K." Sort of redundant, I know. Perhaps that's why they turned on him. I don't know. Now he looks like a stunned cicada, if you know what I mean. And you better know what I mean because you learned what a stunned, dried up cicada looks like in my giant cicada killer wasp 101 class you took from me your sophomore year.

And more fascinating news. For some unknown reason, even to me, a famous expert on giant cicada killer wasps, Feckle's gob of super whoppers traveled southeast to Augusta, and have caused quite a "buzz" there. Just one of the super whoppers, I have been told, cleared out the Wal-Mart.

Therefore, I have been hired by the Augusta Chamber of Commerce to investigate why they chose Augusta, instead of more deserving towns like Siloam or Hephzibah, and what might be done to rid this innocent town of Feckle's beasts. Please consult my Ultimate! and Exclusive! giant cicada killer wasp web site for frequent updates.

Devotees, all I can say at this point is this: humans and cicadas of Augusta, Georgia, watch out. Be very watch out.

■　　■　　■

Waymon's Reaction to Professor Biswapati's Latest News

Visiting the web site did not make Waymon feel better. Not one bit. He did not add "PROFESSOR JEEVPIL BISWAPATI'S ULTIMATE! AND EXCLUSIVE! GIANT CICADA KILLER WASP WEB SITE" to his "Favorites."

Waymon moaned to his computer screen in the eerie quiet of apartment 1931, "Professor Biswapati, sweet *Jeee*-sus, you got to get rid of those dang super whopper thangs by next year's volunteer day... *please*."

PART IV

Waymon: A Curious Review

Garlic Pow-Pow-Power

When Bartwick Dilworth IV was finally made Executive Vice President of Customer Service of TrustTrust Banks, he planned not to brush his teeth, shave, clean or clip his fingernails, toenails, use deodorant, or cleanse his butt crack for four days.

At the dinner table, the evening of his promotion, as a friendly, deeply loving warning, but with a distinct enthusiasm in his voice, Bartwick Dilworth IV announced these intentions to his wife and son.

Xing La La, his wife, thought he had temporarily lost his mind. You don't consciously *not* cleanse your butt crack for four days—actually, you don't consciously *not* cleanse your butt crack for two seconds. You rub on it, from time to time, a mixture of liquefied Chinese herbs with a gauze pad, then meditate.

Dilworth's fourteen-year-old son thought his father's current freaking out situation was totally cool—and finally and totally time for it as he was always such a serious suit dad who worked at some bank shit stuff thing downtown, and eagerly offered a suggestion that in order to get totally skanky he should also eat at least two peeled cloves of garlic before bed, every night, as this would, throughout the next day, make him "crank like a mule."

At this juncture, Dilworth's wife, who was an extremely Americanized, opinionated, and educated big-city woman, who lived in a three-and-a-half-million-dollar mansion with her husband and son, left the table and decided to flee down to Sea Island to their one-and-a-half-million-dollar beach house and her Pilates instructor, with whom she had been experimenting with lesbianism. Xing La La knew what the word "crank" meant and she hated that civilization allowed hyperactive, odd looking, pimpled children—not proper people—to get to add new words to dictionaries.

Wow. Okay then. Bye, Mom.

Anyhow, the kid didn't miss a beat. *Four* cloves, the father was told, in an extremely confidential and business-like tone of voice over his plate of food, would make a person crank like a MARTA bus. *Six* cloves, a 747 jet airplane, or a Howitzer cannon, say. Plus, it was explained by the son, that the cranks would also *smell* like garlic and any doofus who walked into your "smoke trail" would get "knocked *out.*" Plus, *plus*, at this level of exploitation your body will begin to *ooze* garlic crank through your skin and you would also win international awards for your bad breath.

Dilworth was mesmerized by this fascinating information, proven by the fact that he sat there with his mouth open, gazing at his son as if a broiler chicken was crawling out of the child's ear. Dilworth's son was also named Bartwick, and Bartwick V learned of the garlic eating crank thing from his best friend Ralph Jenkins VIII, who was a huge proponent of a nightly, personal "six clove." Bartwick and Ralph are eighth graders at Atlanta's oldest, most expensive, most exclusive, and most prestigious private college preparatory school where they're co-presidents of the Human Physiology Club.

Anyhow, during his promotion that day, Dilworth was informed by the president of TrustTrust that since he was now the new executive vice president of customer service as opposed to his former role as senior vice president of customer service that it was time to really, really come up with some good ideas.

Dilworth said he finally had one that would lead TrustTrust into the customer service future.

The president asked what it was in particular.

Dilworth said he was going to once and for all go check out a Waymon Poodle cat up in Mullet Luv and "bottle" Waymon Poodle and feed it to every employee in all five states and the District of Columbia who had anything to do with customers, as customers and their money, a recent TrustTrust survey revealed, were important.

The president of TrustTrust, who read a huge number of golf magazines in the TrustTrust presidential toilet, in addition to his banking magazines, said wasn't this the Waymon Poodle who was on every cover of every golf magazine—the energetic chap down at the recent Masters who grabbed a woman's Bermuda grass? Dilworth, we don't grab women's Bermuda grasses at TrustTrust, even the Bermuda grass of our wealth management clients—even if they *ask* us to.

Dilworth delicately reminded his chief that Waymon Poodle was an employee of TrustTrust Banks and was also the finest teller in the history of TrustTrust, revealed every year of his employment by the massive TrustTrust customer survey, to be the friendliest and most competent of any teller in any branch in all five states and the District of Columbia in which we did business.

The president of TrustTrust sort of said, "Oh."

"And now that he's famous for grabbing that old woman's Bermuda grass at the Masters," Dilworth chirped, "the Mullet Luv Publix branch is number one in the company. They're lined up to Chattanooga to engage in, and en*joy*, personal *inter*course with *Poodle!*"

"*Di*lworth, watch your language!"

"Chief, Waymon Poodle is bigger than Phil *Mickel*son."

The president of TrustTrust said, "No shit?"

From the April, 2007 issue of Go *Figure*,
the monthly report of the
American Psychological Association

———————

We were intrigued by a recent study of the sex fantasy
concoction activities of young and middle-aged male humans,
which produced unexpected findings relating to golf. A
decision was made to further pursue the psychological effects
of golf as it relates to rational thinking, as this might be
thrilling.

We discovered that no matter how hard it is raining, even
with lightning, onto the premises of a public, private, semi-
private, or resort golf course, and no matter if the Doppler
weather radar clearly shows that it will continue to rain
heavily—even in deluge amounts—for the next several days,
non-stop, like in the Bible that time,
that golfers, as they gaze at the rain and the clouds
and the deadly lightning and even point at it, truly believe
in their hearts that it will stop raining at any moment. And
they can go golf.

Curious Monkey

It was true, Dilworth thought. True. People judge you by the way you look and that wasn't nice at *all*.

He had stepped out of his new "Phoenix Red" three hundred and seventy horsepower, eighty-two-thousand-dollar Jaguar XKR coupe in the Publix parking lot and immediately the old man in the Camry next to told him to get a job. Yeah, his old wife said it too. Get a job. To the tune of that Bruce Hornsby song, no less. Hey, Bartwick's thinking, this was what very special secret corporate responsibility looks like, you know, from time to time. How dare them? If they only knew. I'm Bartwick Dilworth, Executive Vice President of Customer Service of TrustTrust Banks. That's who I am. He snarled back at them. The old man shot him a bird. Dilworth pressed a finger against his left nostril and blew snot out of the right one. But he accidentally blew snot on his Jaguar and not the Camry.

Anyhow.

Of course. Four days of bed hair. The skanky, uneven beard. Bags under his eyes. Butt crack uncleansed. He was special.

On the walkway now in front of the grocery store. Dilworth wearing only one shoe, an old snakeskin cowboy boot. Walking this way made him limp like Quasimodo. Tattered, greasy jeans, with both knees cut open. The top of his underwear showing. Three watches on one arm, eccentric style. One of Xing La La's clip-on earrings hanging off a lobe. The mother snapping up her daughter as he walked by, clutching her child, her back to Dilworth. Frozen. Like she didn't know what to do. Dilworth stopped and gazed at them like a curious monkey until she ran away. Ran. Dilworth lit a cigarette. Hadn't smoked in years and remembered how it made him pause and think, and then get a headache. He thought about Waymon Poodle, as he sucked in the smoke, watching a teenage girl at the outdoor ATM, punching buttons. As if on instinct she turned, looked him up and down. Get a *job*, she said with a sneer, you gross skank.

Thank you, dear.

Dilworth could smell his own breath. Knew when you could smell it yourself it was really bad. And the garlic oozing from his skin, too. You could smell it. Gross as absolute hell but he'd achieved what he wanted, Bartwick Dilworth, really thinking outside the old paw paw patch on this one. Way off to Jupiter on this one. Sure, I could come on in here on Saturday morning, rich guy, smart, casual, clean-shaven, no socks, four-hundred-dollar loafers, and prance up to this cat at his window and inflict the same pain. Customers do it every day. Because they like it, these customer people.

Through the sliding doors now and by the carts, then through the next set of sliding doors.

A Mullet Luv policeman with a package of frozen chicken wings (mild) checking out in lane five looking up at him. Hold everything. The cashier trying to hand the policeman his change but he's glued on this whacko limping into the store. Not bank robber profile, but the kind who cause extensive trouble, especially in the produce section. Just grabbing and eating and they bark at you. Haul them out kicking and screaming about their rights and then they scratch your eyes out and try to spit into your mouth, and then they sue you. Hadn't seen this particular guy around. Just watch him. Don't even let him get started. I could nail him on the cigarette, but...

Dilworth burped at the policeman, then flicked the cigarette into the air. It landed on a plastic grocery bag being filled with groceries and melted through the plastic and fell onto, and into, a three pack of white corn.

Dilworth kept moving. Marlboro Light garlic smoke surrounding his head. Seven cloves last night of the ancient remedy. Used for centuries for ailments, garlic.

Now for opportunity.

And there he was, Waymon Poodle. *Jeeesus.* Just serving up a storm. Facial action and voice like a cartoon. The guy was genetically wired for this shit. One on one. Can do. I'm going to make you happy. And the famous right hand, the one that cupped the Masters Bermuda grass. Unbelievable. Customers waiting in line, fourteen of them, all probably waiting for Poodle. And there's that other Waymon dude, the branch manager, snooping around back there behind the tellers, like he's looking for dirty fingernails.

Sensing something very strange back there behind them, these valued customers. So they turn, just a little, some over their left shoulder where Dilworth could be discreetly glanced at, some over their right shoulder, but not seeing what it was, whatever it was. Just a sense of something, and it wasn't good. Then a glance over their left shoulder and there this thing was. Sort of hanging there. A look on his face like an animal, looking for trouble, mouth hung open, breathing through it.

Then the smell hits them and all fourteen go in different directions.

Now the space between Dilworth and Waymon was about twenty feet. Dilworth hanging there, his weight more on his left side. Now looking right at Waymon.

Wanting him.

Going to mess him up good.

See what he's made of, this Bermuda grass grabber, the future of TrustTrust Banks Incorporated.

Waymon squawked, "Here to help our *next* valued TrustTrust customer to-*day!*"

Exsqueeze Me?

Twenty feet. That's all the distance and time Waymon Poodle needed to say a prayer.

That's right. As this valued customer approached his window, limping, Waymon Poodle asked the Lord God Jesus—even though TrustTrust didn't require its employees to pray for their valued customers; it was totally optional—to bestow on this valued customer the good common sense to take a bath and brush his teeth as it would just really make him feel like a better person. It was actually a prayer Waymon prayed a lot. It wasn't the fear of being held up or having to deal with check fraud every ten minutes of every day. Not at all. Bank tellers around the world had to, in such quiet, professional surroundings, even in a branch in a dang grocery store, deal with untold numbers of valued customers with body odor. Noxious, palpable, warm body odor that wafted in from behind them, then over the counter and into the teller's face and up their nose or onto the tongue of tellers who breathed through their mouth. God love these people, Waymon thought, but they're still the valued customer. And I value them. Even the valued construction workers who are the worst smellers when they come flooding in here on Fridays around three-thirty. And the valued old, retired people who love to engage in teller transactions but who forget to wash for weeks. And the valued people who work in bars. Valued customers with medical-attention quality halitosis. And especially those valued, fitness-conscious customers who've just come from the fitness center without having a post-workout bath, carrying their valued toddler who has a really bad diaper, and more than likely they'll set the toddler up on the counter while they fiddle around in their belly packs, and you can even hear the poo-poo squeeze around in there and ooze out the sides, and then they'll spew vomit on the teller counter and on the nameplates of tellers. You have to unconditionally love this job. And I do. I am Waymon Poodle and I do.

The valued beast was two feet away now, breathing. Breathing hard on purpose. Shooting the odor directly at his target. Decided to save a crank when it really needed to test Poodle's will to live. He was Bartwick Dilworth IV, after all. You don't crank in public, or even in private, unless it's medically required. The executive vice president, pushing the hot air out of his mouth as if he were whistling, but no one was hearing a pretty tune.

Waymon Boner was behind Waymon, fiddling with some papers, pretending not to notice, but it was obvious. His head was leaning that way. Starting to catch some of it. Now squinting. Face puckering.

"Good morning! And welcome to TrustTrust!" Waymon nearly screamed. "How are *you* today?"

Let the games begin.

"Yeah, gimme a double cheese with *rings*."

"A double cheese with rings?"

"A double cheese with *rings*! You don't hear so goddamn good, *do* you?" Dilworth bumped Waymon's nameplate with a knuckle. "Huh? Waymon Pooooood-sucker."

Contact.

Waymon's face contorting for a millisecond. Steady, the incredible teller was telling himself. Trust Jesus on this one. This was still a valuable customer... who needs to brush his teeth and his tongue for an hour. "Sir, actually, I think you might want the deli section of the store, which is located all the way down to your left."

Two seconds of this and Waymon Boner had already had enough. What a scum bag. He nudged up against Waymon's back. "Sir, the deli is *that* way." He pointed that way. "Thank you and have a roast beef day."

"Awright. Forget the cheeseburger, fellas. I'm just gonna reach back there and pinch your *weenies*."

Waymon Boner: "Oh, my *God*."

Waymon Poodle, giggling. What else to do? The valued customer isn't always right, or polite, but by gosh they're still the valued customer even if he says he's going to pinch your weenie. "Sir, this is a bank branch, not one of those—"

"Asian jack shacks?"

"Yessir, one of those. Now, can I perhaps assist you in a transaction?"

Unbelievable. Unflappable. I just asked if I could pinch his weenie. And what eye do you look at?

Dilworth put a rumpled, dirty, half-wet check onto the counter and pushed it forward. The dirty fingernails. The three watches on his arm.

Waymon Boner, riveted, rose over Waymon's shoulder on tip-toes to have a look.

"*Well*, now. Thank you sir," Waymon said as he looked over the check like a machine, but still smiling, still poised like a soldier. Red flags everywhere. Every item was written in a different hand. Made out to "Cashh." The amount: $3.28. Waymon's hand on the teller machine keypad entering the account number. Not even looking at the keypad. Those long famous fingers going a million miles an hour, commenting to this vile, vulgar, valued customer about the weather, how the Braves were playing lately, while the valued customer silently whistled, real hard.

Waymon Boner observing like a trainee, staring at the teller machine screen for the signature verification to come up, then to Waymon's fingers, then back to the screen. The mock account set up by Dilworth days ago with one of those suspicious geeks in operations. Only five dollars in the account belonging to this guy, Willie Wonka. It checked out. Both Waymons let out a sigh of relief. Waymon Boner's sigh of relief through his gaping mouth more obvious than Waymon Poodle's who let it out through his nose. He though it was more polite to do it that way in front of a valued customer, let out sighs through your nose. And his hands still going a million miles an hour, flicking through the cash drawer now: bills, coins, then the little envelope, stuffing the contents into the envelope with a neat flick of the hand then handing the envelope directly to the valued customer's hand. Never placing the envelope on the counter and pushing it at them as if you thought the valued customer was unwashed. Never distancing himself from the valued customer. He'd reach across the counter and pat them on the back if they'd let him.

Mr. Wonka, on purpose, poured the money onto the counter and took his time counting it.

Now a semi-circle of valued customers, Waymon Poodle fans all, had re-assembled, watching. Some on tiptoe, some smiling. Some touching their lips with anticipation, some whispering to each other. The Mullet Luv policeman at the magazine rack now and had a good line of sight, right hand near his pistol; a Maxim in the other. It was the Jennifer Lopez, 1,456 sex positions, and fantastic buns in seconds issue.

"What a *pleasure* it is serving you today, Mr. Wonka," Waymon purred as he waited for Mr. Wonka to finish, thinking that's exactly the name of the guy who owned that chocolate factory in that movie and who ended up giving it to that little boy or the purple girl or whoever. "Yessir. It certainly is good to *see* you." Waymon, instinctively, turned his nameplate a little bit more toward Mr. Wonka. Waymon took a deep, cleansing breath.

Mr. Wonka was really taking his time.

"Everything seem to be in order, Mr. Wonka?"

"Fuck. I need one more penny."

Waymon Boner: "No, *sir*, you chocolate maker. Now you take your three dollars and twenty-eight cents and go to the deli section and pinch those guy's weenies down *there.*"

"It's quite all right, gentlemen," Waymon said with a cordial lilt. "I certainly could have miscounted. It's quite possible I did." He didn't. Instead of recounting the money himself, Waymon reached into the cash drawer and pulled out a penny and handed it to Mr. Wonka. "*Here* you go."

Mr. Wonka took the penny from Waymon, swallowed it, and then burped.

A burp like the breath of a petting zoo llama.

Meaty, with heat and force behind it.

It smelled of nothing of this earth.

Waymon Boner, running toward the break room: "I'm going to totally *puke.*"

Waymon Poodle, breathing it all in. No reaction, just a smile. "Mr. Wonka, what *else* can I do for you to-day?"

Dumb question. Mr. Wonka was just getting warmed up.

Iceberg. Beware

Carmalita was filing Dilworth's toenails.

He was smoking a big cigar and watching her brown little Venezuelan hand *zip–zip–zip* with a silver nail file on the end of his big toe's big thick, cream-yellow toenail. Dilworth and Carmalita were in the sun room, on a lazy Saturday afternoon: Carmalita, their long-time manicurist who made house calls, and thick white cigar smoke hanging around them.

It was the smoke from a victory cigar.

Dilworth pointed at the portable phone by her arm. "Baby doll, would you hand me the phone?"

She didn't speak English. She kissed his big toe. Then bit it and winked.

"No, no, sugar." He made a hand gesture by his ear, then pointed at it again. "The *tele*–phone."

"*Ah.*" She handed it to him then went back to town on the toe. She had already done his fingernails and shaved him and clipped his hair. Dilworth loved women from international countries. It was a swanky scene.

Dilworth dialed the bank branch he had molested that morning. Fourteen rings. Not good.

"Thank you for calling TrustTrust Bank, conveniently located in the Publix grocery store in Mullet Luv, Georgia. How may I *help* you?"

"Waymon Boner, please."

"Oh, it's pronounced Bo-*nay*, actually. And how may I *help* you?"

"Bo-nay? *French?*"

An audible huff. "Pretty sure. French. And *your name?*"

"Bartwick *Dilworth.* American."

Waymon's eyes widened. Oh *shit.* One of the suits. Calling on a Saturday? "Oh, yes, indeeed, Mr. Dilworth. So how's everything at the old… *headquarters?*"

"*Not* good."

"Not good?"

"*Not* good. I got an upset Mr. Wonka here."

Waymon's heart dropped. "I'd like to explain exactly what happened.

He was a horrible and total stink—"

"But a valued *cus*tomer, nonetheless." Dilworth giggled under his breath.

"Well, if I can be forthright about the situation, the man was a horrible and total stinky freak out."

"A horrible and total stinky *freak out?*"

"Yes, he *was*. Very much a horrible and total stinky *freak* out." Waymon was already sweating by this point. Big drops. He couldn't catch his breath.

"But Mr. Wonka is a valued customer, Waymon. A valued customer."

"But Mr. Dilworth, he *breathed* on me."

"He was your valued customer?"

"Well, not exactly. I ob*serrr*ved the entire freak out."

"The teller's name is Waymon, too, I think, according to Mr. Wonka, who's very upset." Dilworth winked at Carmalita.

Waymon leaned over and looked through his glass office door at Waymon at his window. Now they were getting somewhere. "*Right*. That's the Waymon. Does he need to work for me any longer Mr. Dilworth, sir, if you know what I *mean?*"

"Actually, I can't decide what to do with him. Give him a promotion or the employee of the year award or *both*."

"Excuse me?"

"You saw how he handled Mr. Wonka. You were standing right there."

Waymon squinted. "How do you know *that?*"

"I was Mr. Wonka. *Sort* of."

Waymon dropped the phone.

It was loud. Dilworth scrunched his face up.

Carmalita bit his big toe again.

"So very sorry, sir. You really were Mister Wo—"

"Just tell me something about Poodle."

"Yessir. *Really* sorry. But you really were Mister Wo—"

"Shut up a second."

"Yessir." A big drop of sweat dropped into the sour cream on Waymon's burrito.

"What's the one big thing Poodle wants out of his career? His performance was incredible."

"*Well*, Mr. Dilworth. Believe it or not, he really is content to be a teller.

He really does like customers."

Dilworth rolled his eyes.

"See"—Waymon sighed for about six seconds—"his whole big life *goal* thing is to play golf at Augusta Country Club."

"Augusta *Country* Club? Good *God. Why?*"

"You know, where they play the U.S. Open or whatever."

"Oh, Augusta *National*. The *Masters*."

"Like I said. What-*everrrr*."

"You're kidding me."

"I swear to God. That's all he *lives* for. Except who knows if it'll ever come true *now*, *you* know, since on TV he grabbed that woman's—*Oh*, and I guess you know his big volunteer day was totally wiped out by the wrath of God—his words. So he's still squirming to play Augusta National Country Club. Just squirming, squirming, *squirming*, Waymon *Poodle*."

"*Squir*ming, huh?"

"Listen, Mr. Dilworth, you could promote Waymon Poodle to executive vice president—"

"Watch it now."

"—but if he could play that golf course nothing in the world would make him happier. I mean, really. You saw that hideous tie he was wearing."

"*Yeah*."

"Well, sir, he's wears it every single *day*."

"No kidding."

"Be very afraid, Mr. Dilworth, that's just the *tip* of his iceberg."

Kidding Aside

It was 5:30 in the morning on Monday and Bartwick Dilworth was peeking into the office of the president of TrustTrust Banks with a big smile on his face.

The president was sitting back in his chair with a big smile on his face.

The reason they're doing all this smiling at each other at 5:30 in the morning, as opposed to any other time of the day, was that the TrustTrust public relations guy suggested that if all the bank big shots were to get to work at 5:30 in the morning, and if they could get some articles published in the newspaper and some magazines and maybe have a local television station do a story about how the "bank's leaders" arrived at 5:30 every morning because "they cared about you" as opposed to getting there at the crack of dawn because they wanted to beat traffic, then this would increase business and create a feeling of goodwill in the community. Bank big shots being seen and reported in the newspaper to have run in marathons was also suggested. On the day the article appeared in the newspaper about how they cared about you, three million people created new accounts at TrustTrust. So everybody was real happy.

But Dilworth and the president really weren't smiling because of that. They hated to have to get to work every day at 5:30. They were smiling because word had already gotten around the home office and on the TrustTrust intranet chat rooms about what some downtown muckety-muck did at the Mullet Luv, Georgia/Publix branch on Saturday and the teller dweeb, everyone agreed, whose basic civil rights were violated, and how wild it got and how well the teller fended off the scum bag with great service and a smile. It was concluded by the employees who spent an inordinate amount of time typing up chat room letters to each other as opposed to performing their duties, that the teller won: Waymon Poodle of the Mullet Luv, Georgia/Publix branch. He was the winner.

A banner crawled across the bottom of every computer screen of every TrustTrust employee in all five states and the District of Columbia with this announcement: Way to go Waymon!

No one knew that at 5:30 every morning the president of TrustTrust

Banks read the chat room comments for kicks. "Ah," the president said with a satisfied tone, "Mr. *Wonka*. Come right in."

Dilworth walked in and sat down. It was a large office so it took him a while to get there. "*Big* news, chief."

"Give me the nutshell, Dilworth. I'm a busy man."

"It's five-thirty in the morning. How in the hell are you busy?"

"Hey, I finally decided to try to make the coffee as a gesture of good-will to other people who work here. I've never made office coffee in my *life*. Dilworth, you want some advice now that you're up here with the big shots?"

"Fuck. I *guess*."

"Just press the goddamn coffee machine start button *once*."

"*Yes*, chief."

"So, did you smell really bad?"

"Like a six-pound poo-poo diaper. Remember those?"

"Outstanding, Dilworth. But you know ol' Wonkka down in public relations is upset you used his name."

"He's got an extra 'k' in his name, right? W-o-n-k-*k*-a?"

"Hell, I *think* so. It's not like I sit up here on the tenth floor all day counting the letters in emplo—"

"Well, I *don't* have an extra 'k.' W-o-n-k-*a*."

"Brilliant stroke, Dilworth. Goddamn brilliant. How long did the transaction take?"

"Two and half hours."

"Jesus! You're kidding me."

"I'm not kidding. I'm pretty darn sure it's a company record. I got my mortgage refinanced. He reconciled my checkbook. And he showed me how to pay my bills online. The most incredible thing I've ever seen in my life—while I was emitting gross flatulence from my butthole the entire time and licking his nameplate with my tongue."

"Brilliant stroke, Dilworth. Brilliant. So he's our *man*, huh? And you've bottled him?"

"I'm typing up a big memo this morning, or one of my secretaries is. We're going to completely change the way we conduct business at the windows just because of this guy Waymon Poodle. We're going to be nice as shit to *everybody*."

"All this in the budget?"

"No."

"Oh."

"But *chief*, there's one thing we've got to do for him, but I don't know if we can pull it off. It's a little weird."

"What's weird?"

"I called the branch manager and asked him what Poodle really wanted out of life and it has nothing to do with pecking up the ol' TrustTrust ladder. He's content to stay a teller."

"That's terrible."

"Here's all he wants out of life. This cat's life goal is to play Augusta."

The president made a face. "Augusta? Augusta *Country Club?*"

"God, no. Augusta *National.*"

"You're kidding me."

"Hey! We've got some customers who are members, don't we?"

The president of TrustTrust looked to his left, then to his right as if he were looking to see if anyone else was in his office, then mouthed, "*I'm* a member."

"What? Speak up." Dilworth leaned toward him.

He mouthed it again. "*I'm* a member." Then he fluffed his tie. An Augusta National Golf Club tie, just like the one Waymon wears to work every day. And to church.

"You're kidding me."

"No, I'm not."

"How come you never *told* me?"

"Look around my office, Dilworth."

Dilworth looked around the president's office. The walls were covered with prints of Augusta National Golf Club holes. Framed flags with invitee signatures. Hole-in-one balls under niche lights. "Chief, every booger eatin' Masters nerd in the *world* has this fake shit."

"Well, *see*, that's how guys like us, you know, *members*, keep it a secret. We all act like wannabees. But I'll tell you something, Dilworth, they don't want you to tell anybody you're a member."

"They? They *who?*"

"They. You know—*they.*"

"*Oh.*"

"I swear to God. After you get in they have this super secret real big special meeting with you late at night about not telling people you're a member. And now, because I told you, I gotta put a *cap* in yo ass."

They both laughed it up. Really laughed it up.

Dilworth secretly wanted to play too, so he kept pressing. "So let's do it then. Hey, all these consultants are saying we give employees movie tickets and carpal tunnel massages and crap like that even though they're doing their job anyway. Augusta National. Now that's a real reward."

"Well, sure, Dilworth, you *dumb* ass. But this Poodle is real strange looking. Plus I don't think I want to show up on the first tee in front of all my other members with the guy who grabbed our club receptionist's Bermuda grass. Hell, he's probably already played in the thing they have for all those volunteers so we're off the hook. So get back to work."

"Volunteer day got rained *out*."

"Well it's not *my* fault. Members of Augusta National Golf Club don't have any control over the *weather*." The president winked.

"Chief, that's the day the hallowed back nine floated away. I heard the twelfth green got washed to Siloam."

"*What!*"

"You're a member and you didn't *know?*"

"Well I'm sure our fine golf course maintenance staff will *fix* it. My God. Close your eyes, Dilworth."

"Close my eyes for *what?*"

"So you won't see where I keep my member newsletter. I swear to God. After you get in they have this super secret real big special meeting with you late at night about not letting people see where you keep your member newsletter."

"You're kidding me."

"Shut up. Now close your eyes."

Dilworth barely closed his eyes.

The president kept his newsletter under his toupee. "All right. Yep. Says right here they fixed it the other day. The twelfth green is as good as new except… *huh?*"

"*What?*"

"Says here we're still missing a chunk of the green and the microchip in the chunk says it's somewhere—good *God*—in *Mullet* Luv. Get a load of *that*, somewhere in goddamn Mullet Luv. Now that's really a hopping place. I've got to get *up* there sometime. Hey Dilworth!"

"Sir!"

"*Cap* in yo ass. That was a *good* one."

Dilworth chuckled then made a strange expression.

"What, *now?* Quit chuckling and then making strange expressions. Get outta here."

"Chief, we gotta *do* something for this guy. We can play when the club reopens in the fall, *right?*"

"*We?*"

"Yeah, *we.* You, me, and *Poodle,* and whoever *else* you pick."

"Listen, just promote him to branch manager or something. Go give him a carpal tunnel massage."

"All he wants is to play Augusta Country Club. Jeeesus! Augusta National. And so do I."

"Fine. *God.* You can play. You're acting like a little kid, Dilworth."

"Well, this is what this thing *does* to people."

"Then call him up. Get him down here. We'll tell him he can play Augusta National and see if he shits."

Dilworth looked at his watch. "It's five forty-two in the *morning!*"

"If he's the bank's savior then he's probably sitting there waiting on the first valued customer to arrive—in the *dark!* And get up off your knees."

"But one more thing, chief."

"I'm *sure* I told you to get outta here."

In the presidential office suite of the president of TrustTrust Banks, Bartwick Dilworth rose from his Augusta National Golf Club begging position, turned around, and after pushing an Augusta National Golf Club paper weight to the side, hiked his rear end upon the enormous Brazilian cherry desk of the president of TrustTrust Banks then pulled the back of his jacket up.

"*Dilworth,*" the president barked, "what the hell are you *doing?*"

"Chief, I saved the *big* one for you, from Saturday."

"*Saved* one. Saved *what* big one in God's name? *Dilworth!*"

"It's *Wonka,* chief. Garlic clove abuser, and it's harvest time."

Air Waymon

The president of TrustTrust was right. Sort of.

Publix are open twenty-four hours a day so if he was at his teller window right then he wouldn't have been, technically, in the dark. Waymon was in the dark at that moment, however, the dark of apartment 1931. But the keypad of his green phone was brightly lit.

Beginning at 6:00 each morning Waymon began checking the branch's voice mails as he lay in bed. This was his idea.

It didn't take long for Waymon, who was, obnoxiously, the first to arrive every morning, to discover that valued customers often left voice mails in the middle of the night. Most of them were profanity-laced complaints concerning other banks, but every now and then, a valued customer might leave a reasonable question or a great idea the bank could use without the insistence of compensation. So Waymon decided to check the voice mails beginning at the crack of dawn each day. It thrilled Waymon to no end to ponder a valued customer's question or request while he took his shower and drove to the branch so he'd be prepared to call the valued customer the moment he got to the branch and give them the absolute best and correct answer according to Waymon Poodle and TrustTrust Banks. Of course, calling back valued customers was Waymon Boner's responsibility but he happily allowed Waymon the opportunity to enhance his customer service skills as Waymon seemed real freaked out to want to do it.

Waymon got an interesting message this morning that had been left at 5:45: A Bartwick Dilworth, Executive Vice President of Customer Service and the president of TrustTrust would like to see him downtown this morning as soon as possible. Okay, Waymon? Real important so soon as possible. Just come on down some time before lunch to the president's office. Tenth floor. Thanks. Have a nice day.

"Lord God Jesus," Waymon breathed. Then hit the "2" button to replay it.

By car, from Mullet Luv to downtown Atlanta, was eighty-one miles and it usually takes almost two hours to get to Atlanta. Then you gotta throw in the traffic.

Of course, then you've got to find a parking space in one of those spooky parking decks and as you make your way to the building you've got to fend off homeless people and street preachers who pose complex philosophical or religious questions to you and follow you down the sidewalk or across the park until you give them an answer which is never correct in their opinion, even if it actually is the correct answer. This was once Waymon's personal experience. Of course, he could take the MARTA train but MARTA trains made him claustrophobic, especially when they went underground.

So instead of turning left out of the Sans Souci apartments toward Atlanta, Waymon Poodle, smiling, because he knew getting there real quick was the right thing to do as you never get called downtown by these people unless it's real bad or real good, not in between he had heard, turned right and drove half a mile to the Mullet Luv Helicopter Center. Come to find out the parking lot of the Mullet Luv Helicopter Center was already full of huge Mercedes and Dodge Vipers and Ferraris because Waymon discovered as he boarded a shiny green (an omen) helicopter, it was full of rich-type people who lived up there in Mullet Luv in some of those new rich-type neighborhoods and who refused to sit in Atlanta traffic and were willing to pay $150 per day, per round trip, weather permitting. They were all reading *Wall Street Journals* and golf magazines, more omens.

It was 6:08.

Waymon poked his head into the door of the president of TrustTrust Banks at 6:21. The seven secretaries weren't there yet, so that's how he got in.

The president cheerfully said to Waymon that his office had already been vacuumed and wiped off and whatnot. But thank you nonetheless and go away and have a nice day.

"Sir," Waymon said. "You and Mr. Dilworth wanted to see me?"

The president made a strange expression. "And you *are?*"

"Waymon Poodle. Waymon Poodle of the Mullet Luv Publix branch."

The president looked around his office as if he were trying to find a prankster hiding behind one of his five sofas. Then he looked at his watch "How—?"

"I took a helicopter. I thought I should get here as quick as I *could.*"

Although Waymon was sweating and his personal presentation arresting, even more so at 6:21 in the morning, the president walked toward Waymon with an expression of fear and appreciation all mixed together and wrapped an arm around his shoulder and led him to a chair, then whacked Waymon on the back. "You're an amazing animal, Waymon. Truly one of a kind of a human being. So good to *meet* you I think."

"*Thank* you." Waymon sat down.

"Now I mean that as a compliment."

"You bet, sir."

The president lurched forward and pointed. "Hey, I like your tie!"

"Hey, yours, too, sir."

They both smiled at each other and held their Augusta National Golf Club-logoed ties in their hands and looked at each other's ties and smiled some more and essentially had a moment together. Then the president cleared his throat and called Dilworth on the phone.

"Good morning, Bartwick Dilworth the fourth, Executive Vice President of Customer Service of TrustTrust Banks. Thank you for calling. And how in the world can I help *you* today with *your* problem?"

The president cupped a hand over his mouth and whispered. "Cut the *shit*, Dilworth. You're not gonna believe who's sitting in my office at this very moment."

"Wonkka?"

"No, dumb ass—*Poodle*."

"No *way*. I just left a message at his branch not two minutes ago."

"He took a goddamn *helicopter*."

"Kiss my *ass*. He knows how to fly a helicopter, *too?*"

"*Dilworth*," the president said, "hang on a second."

"*Right!*"

"Uh, *Waymon*. Where's the helicopter now?"

"On the roof, waiting for me. There's a helicopter pad up there."

"*Really?*"

"Right up there on the roof."

"I did not *know* that. Well I'll be—Dilworth."

"*Yes*, chief!"

"Get *down* here."

"*Right!*"

While they waited for Dilworth, Waymon and the president fiddled with their ties and looked at each other, smiling uneasily.

The door opened.

"Ah, *Dilworth!*" The president shouted. "Waymon, do you recognize this fellow here?"

Waymon shook Dilworth's hand and smiled, as he was a very polite person, but had to admit he did not.

"Waymon, you met him Saturday at your branch. You had personal intercourse with him. A lot."

Waymon squinted a little harder. "Sir, I serve with joy an enormous number of valued customers every day, and I deeply apologize for not recognizing him. But I'll certainly make it a point to recognize him next time. Thank you."

Amazing.

"Well, Waymon, I'll just cut to the ol' chase here as we're all busy people doing things. Dilworth here put you on the spot Saturday and you passed an extremely difficult test."

Waymon's eyes widened. He looked at Dilworth and seemed as if he wanted to speak.

Dilworth whistled a silent tune.

Waymon's eyes widened some more.

"That's *right*, Waymon. But let's not rehash all the unpleasantness."

Waymon gazed at Dilworth with an odd look of admiration. "Lordy. Lord God Jesus in Heaven."

"Uhhhh, *right*. Now Waymon, let me ask you a question."

"Yessir."

"What could we do to reward you for your years of serving the needs of our valued customers? Especially Saturday. We'd like to promote you to branch manager or something."

Dilworth butted in. "Hey, I thought we were gonna go play—"

The president held his hand up.

Waymon straightened himself and took a big breath. "Sir, my life goal is—"

"Yes?"

"To *not* be a branch manager so that I can continue to serve, one on one, my valued customers in a face-to-*face*-type way."

"Waymon, *really*," the president said. "Get a grip here. I know there's something *else* you want. Now tell me what it is. Let's be official about this, so… so stand up."

Waymon stood up, but looked at his feet. "It's embarrassing."

"You can tell *me*. I'm your new *pal*. And stand up a little straighter!"

Waymon jerked his shoulders back. "Well, one day it's the most important thing in my life and the next day God punishes me for it. It's called desire, sir."

"Desire for what? Some Bermuda grass?"

"No, sir. Actually, I could have some of that anytime I wanted."

Dilworth said stupidly, "Hey, way to go Way—"

"Shut up, *Dilworth!*"

"*Right!*"

"Sir, I simply desire to play Augusta National Golf Club one time before I die." Waymon took another big breath and looked as if he might cry.

"All *right. Now* we're getting somewhere, Waymon. Okay, now, how does Saturday, October the sixth sound, my boy? The first day of the season and the very first tee time." Puff-chested, the president said, "I give you Augusta Country Club."

Waymon's heart dropped.

"I mean Augusta National, you know, *Golf* Club. *That* one. Sorry."

Waymon touched his head as if he had a sudden pain.

The president whacked Waymon on the back. "Just you and me and a couple of caddies. We'll have a great time. Just get there Saturday morning in time to hit a couple of warm-up balls." The president pretended to hit a warm-up ball.

"*Sir,*" Dilworth croaked.

"What *now?* Thus endeth my goddamn remarks, o-*kay?*"

Dilworth made a goofy expression.

"Oh, *yeah,* and Dilworth here. He might go, too." The president rubbed his hands together and produced some pretty obvious body language that communicated, unequivocally, that the meeting was over and for them to get out. Then, when Dilworth and Waymon didn't get it, the president pushed them toward the door from behind. "Okay? Everybody okay with that date? Super *du*per. You fellows have a great summer—happy Fourth of July and Flag Day and Rosh Hashanah and Labor Day—and we'll see you *then.*" He started to close the door.

Waymon suddenly stopped and the door hit him on the back. "Sir, I might have a slight problem." He touched his head again. This time the pain was real.

"*Waymon?* Your life goal we're talking about here. How slight can it *be?*"

"That's my wedding date."

The president whacked Waymon on the back. "Waymon, *nobody* gets married in October. You get married in June."

"Yeah, *Waymon*. You get married in *June*," Dilworth said.

"Shut *up*, Dilworth," the president said.

"*Right!*"

Waymon said, "She's real headstrong, LaJuanita."

The president grinned. "La-wa-*nee*-ta?

"LaJuanita. LaJuanita Mumps."

"Sounds like she'd have some big *hair*, ol' LaJuanita," the president said. "She got some big *hair*, Waymon? Know what I *mean*?" Credentials? Does LaJuanita have credentials?"

"She sure does, sir," Waymon said stupidly. He had no idea what the man was talking about.

The president squinted at Waymon. "I don't think you know what I *mean*, Waymon. This is hard *work*, communicating with you."

"She's just really got it going on, sir. She really, really does." Waymon felt like he hadn't breathed in the last fifteen minutes. His heart was racing like a sewing machine.

"*So*, Waymon. She play golf, *too*?" The president made another golf swing. He would have shanked it.

"Gosh, *no*. She thinks the wonderful sport of golf in general and the iniquitous allure of what goes on behind the gates of ootsie-tootsie private golf clubs are for flaming squids, bald fat farts, and mules."

Dilworth made a goofy face. "Say, what does iniquit—"

"Well, *hell*," the president bellowed, then pushed Dilworth out of the way and whacked Waymon on the back, "Ol' LaJuanita's goddamn *right!*" The president began laughing so hard he ran out of air, then grabbed his throat with both hands so violently his toupee changed angles and his Augusta National Golf Club member newsletter slipped out and lodged into the cuff of his pants, and then he stumbled around his office knocking over chairs, some little tables, and three floor lamps, and then finally pulled down a nice set of Masters-logoed drapes.

In this delicate moment, Waymon and Dilworth thought the best course of action was to run away.

A Purrsuasion

LaJuanita understood. Completely. Sure she did. Twelve years of hair-dressing taught her a whole lot about mullets and human nature.

Waymon had figured it would be best to go ahead and tell her the news that night since the excitement of it would come through in his voice and mannerisms and facial expressions with great passion: Waymon Poodle had another definite date with Augusta National Golf Club. This one felt for real. It really did.

He had practiced what he was going to say to her in the bathroom mirror and Waymon thought it looked and sounded pretty good. So he lured her over to apartment 1931 with Wendy's food. LaJuanita loved Wendy's food. LaJuanita especially loved a Wendy's double with cheese and everything else and thought she looked sexy when some of the gook that got squeezed out of the cheeseburger ran down her neck and arms and sometimes onto her chest and between her boobs. LaJuanita was wrong about that, but that's what she thought. Waymon appreciated it when LaJuanita ate Wendy's cheeseburgers over his sink or bathtub or even the commode, but she never would.

Just a second after Waymon hit her with the thing about meeting the president of the bank and him being a member and him being real proud of me and my teller work and him being a member (he purposely repeated that part) of Augusta National Golf Club and the business about the first tee time on the first day of the season and how that was also their wedding date and how he felt like he ought to do what the president of the bank told him to do and that was to play golf with him, then LaJuanita's mind went into quick action. She took a big bite out of the double. Then she said, while chewing, that, all right, they could change the date to the next Saturday if Waymon would do one thing for her that evening and any other time she wanted it.

Waymon asked what she wanted, you know, him to do. Asking this question made him very nervous.

Even though LaJuanita was thoroughly "experienced," there was still something about Waymon that turned her on to the highest degree.

Particularly the fact that he had a steady job with a big fancy company and that he wanted to have fourteen kids, too.

Waymon asked her again what it was she wanted him to do as she was really making that Wendy's double disappear and wasn't answering his question.

LaJuanita said that she wanted Waymon to finally fornicate with her, but after she finished eating, and then he could go play golf at Augusta Country Club on their wedding day.

Well now.

Waymon, using everything he had learned beginning from vacation Bible school to the current lessons he obtained in Sunday School and all the sermons he'd ever heard in his life and watched on TV and most of the stuff he read in the Bible, especially Job, had to quickly rationalize how God might beat the hell out of him if he fornicated with LaJuanita, even if he didn't enjoy it.

The thought—fornication—did actually interest him. Waymon was Waymon, sure, but he wasn't a cave monk. He had been told once, by a nurse, that his pecker was one of the biggest she'd ever seen.

LaJuanita could tell that Waymon was really sorting this one out as she started in on the fries. Eight or nine shoved in there at a time. "Whatcha... th... ink?" she said with two good hiccups. She was eating that cheeseburger too fast. "We're definitely getting married, so it's... ooooo... kay. I've been saying this to you for the last six months. If you don't want to get married then let's not fornicate and I'll just go off and fornicate with soooooomebody named Ken... or something. Or some fucker named Mitch." Then LaJuanita burped. She'd been drinking Miller Lite in cans all afternoon, too, but God forbid if Waymon found out.

Waymon didn't quite understand the logic of fornication. But he did understand his destiny. There had been too many omens. The president of his company, a member no less of Augusta National Golf Club, has made official plans and has official expectations that I will be there at the official appointed time and tee. So Waymon said, officially, "Let's do it."

"Do *what?*"

"What do you mean 'do *what?*'"

"I'm just making sure you... wanna... do it," LaJuanita hiccuped, then burped, then hiccuped again.

"I wanna *do* it."

"I wanna finish my fooooood."

"Finish your food and we'll *do* it."

"But I wanna take a shower first, because I'm nasty down there. I'll get all hot and steamy, then you come on in the bathroom real slow and sexy and take off your clothes and wiggle yourself around while I *watch*." LaJuanita chewed for a moment. "Waymon, honey?"

"Yes, LaJuanita," Waymon said flatly as he was thinking that the correct shot was to fade it around Tea Olive's fairway bunker and not try to hit it right to left because if it didn't turn *left* for some reason you're dead in the bunker.

"Then, like in them sex movies," LaJuanita said. "You come on in there and soap up my boobs."

Doin' It

After Waymon frantically fornicated with LaJuanita, she left to go out to some bars with a bunch of friends.

Waymon went into the second bedroom and shut the door behind him. Because Waymon felt guilty about fornicating with LaJuanita and making her scream a lot, he felt he should punish himself. He turned his computer on, pulled up the Internet, and typed in that certain address given to him by his Christian psychologist, then hit Search. Shakily, wearily, and with extreme tension.

PROFESSOR JEEVPIL BISWAPATI'S ULTIMATE!
AND EXCLUSIVE!
GIANT CICADA KILLER WASP WEB SITE

....

http://www.georgiainstituteoftechnology.edu/Entomology/~biswapati/KILLER.html

....

July 2007

Yes, my devotees, entomology pays. I told you! Yes, I did! Pays good!

Last evening at the Washington Road Hooters I used a little bit of my $800,000 "Super Whopper Location and Elimination" grant given to me by the Augusta Chamber of Commerce. If you have not been to one of these unique dining establishments then allow me to tell you that it is hard to concentrate on your chicken wings.

I felt I stood out from the local patrons and perhaps was perceived as strange by my Hooters food and beverage servant, Pam. She asked me what I was up to in this part of town and after I told her she said, "Creee-peee." I cannot blame Pam. I am creeped out by my discoveries here. That goddamn Feckle.

As you know, I believe nothing is more beautiful than to see a giant cicada killer wasp drag a stunned cicada into its humid burrow, then suck its juices out. It is the same feeling I had watching my eleven children gain freedom from the humid womb. But this is no longer beautiful, my devotees. It is not beautiful to see a Lamar Feckle super whopper drag a cocker spaniel or a flapping chicken into its lair. And then to hear their screams.

Upon meeting with the nice people of the Augusta Chamber of Commerce, I stuck the check into a hole in my saree then asked them where might I find expansive areas of sandy, well drained soil in full sunlight in Augusta, Georgia, as this is where the super whoppers would have certainly ended up. I was directed to a place called Augusta National Golf Club. This is where Feckle's gob have come to roost and pulsate.

I have once seen a golf course in a magazine, but this is not at all what I expected. I understand that wealthy men with prominent bellies and turkey necks follow around a little white ball and attempt to loft the ball into the air with a titanium device called a "club" onto a "green." A most difficult endeavor this golf must be. At Augusta National Golf Club the greens are protected by tents that must, I think, be used to deflect the balls into "traps of sand." Bulldozers also roam the golf course scooping up large wads of grass and dirt. Bodies of water are deliberately re-routed in an attempt to frustrate the man who is golfing. Large tree-planting machines scoop up various trees—some over 300 feet tall—and move them only inches from where they once stood. Loud helicopters constantly fly over the golf course with photographers taking photographs of these various activities. Certain of these aforementioned greens are also dug up and replaced on exactly the place where they once were! They say they are "proofing" the course for a "tiger." I have not come to this place for tigers. I do not understand.

But this I understand: the caretakers of this golf course, who constantly chew and spit tobacco-laden saliva streams into the air and smoke Marlboro Lights—at the same time—are very nervous. Feckle's gob have chosen as their base of destruction and horror a place called the "twelfth tee," noted by the locals to be hallowed. These caretakers are meaty, sunburned men, but they are afraid of this twelfth tee and the perverted creatures that roam and rule the air space above, and below, this grass, or in their unique vernacular, "turf." Super whopper elimination is simple work, I have informed them. Take a tennis racket down there and whack the shit out of them. I'll watch from here. "Toby done tried that," one meaty fellow retorted. "And Toby ain't never come back yet."

Toby, I know, is being cuddled in the arms of the mukhya nyayadhish. I, Jeevpil Biswapati, must regroup and earn my cabbage, as the tennis racket idea is my best one. But I am also confused and afraid. I must ponder what drastic action to take. Over another bucket of chicken wings at Hooters.

■　■　■

Waymon's Reaction to
Professor Biswapati's Latest News

Talking to his computer screen in the eerie quiet of apartment 1931: "Professor Biswapati. You gotta get those thangs by October *sixth*.

Oh my *Lord*.

PART V

Summer of Soap

Sweat Equity

So there was Waymon, all summer long soaping up LaJuanita's boobs and fornicating and trying as hard as he could not to daydream about super whopper giant cicada killer wasps at Augusta National Golf Club.

It was a long summer.

Waymon discovered that LaJuanita enjoyed fornication with all the covers kicked down to the end of the bed and Waymon, covered with goose bumps, wearing a purple Trojan "Magnum XL" condom covered with pleasure knobs the size of pencil erasers, on top of her for a while—over her, really—as if he were doing push ups, then she'd flip over and Waymon would fornicate for a while that way, then she'd flip over again and finish on up. LaJuanita never knew when Waymon was finishing on up as he never announced when he was finishing on up or made any finishing on up-type noises. He was so business-like about it.

LaJuanita wasn't so creative herself, but Waymon didn't know otherwise. Her key mid-fornication phrases, delivered in a fairly monotone tone of voice, while she stared at the ceiling fan's pull cord over Waymon's shoulder, were, "Give it to me, Waymon," and "That's the way… Waymon… to give it… to me."

LaJuanita, after a few sessions of fornicating, finally said to Waymon, "I finally figgerd out when you finish on up because you twist up yer face all funny when you finish on up. You oughta look at yerself in a mirror."

Fine, so I twist my face up. You burp and claw your fingernails all over my back.

While fornicating, Waymon would occasionally glance over at his Bible on the night stand and shake his head in shame and shaking his head would usually make a big drop of sweat fall off his nose and hit LaJuanita in the face, which sometimes was okay and sometimes not okay because it depended on the status of her makeup and if she had somewhere else to go after they fornicated whereas her makeup needed to be on right.

What really bothered Waymon the most about all this was that after the front nine he was always five over and it seemed that his approach shot placement was getting him into trouble. You had to stick it near the pin,

Waymon knew, or otherwise you were looking for trouble. Ten, Camellia, was a tough hole for him as it was for a lot of the invitees and he never seemed to have that much trouble with Azalea, but being eight over after Azalea got Waymon worried because there were still some tough holes ahead, like Holly. So when LaJuanita would flip over, Waymon would start back at two, Pink Dogwood, as he always birdied Tea Olive, and try to get his drive a little farther over to the right so he'd have a clear second shot, but not in that fairway bunker. They had moved the tee back, Waymon knew, so he could really beat it down there, but that bunker was always in his mind's eye. Waymon loved the third shot on Pink Dogwood, usually with a lob wedge, to the second green.

LaJuanita yawned. She looked over at the clock radio.

Waymon knew there were two bunkers up there by the green but they didn't bother him. It was definitely a birdie hole. Then one evening, Waymon cold shanked his third shot on Pink Dogwood with his lob wedge, and that's all he needed to push him toward lessons. His secondary goal was to break the course record at Augusta National Golf Club and be well known for that and maybe after he did, Nick Price, the current record co-holder, might call him up from South Africa and Greg Norman from Australia, the other current record co-holder, and congratulate him. Wow, the course record. It could happen. Could. They would up and call him.

That meant shooting a sixty-two. That meant he needed some help. That meant he needed some lessons. Some lessons now.

LaJuanita, lying there, squirming a little bit, staring at the pull cord, while Waymon humped like a piston, finally said that she finished on up about twenty minutes ago and she'd appreciate it if he would too.

Blind Devotion

The Wednesday night scene at the Mullet Luv Golf Center was frightening to an outsider, mostly out of town business guys staying at local hotels who come over to whack a few balls in their expensive logoed golf shirts from their home clubs or some resort they took the wife and kids to or the golf courses near where they had a trade show. They have to make a quick decision once they walk through the door whether to proceed to the counter. Most do not proceed. The facility does not smell nice.

But for the regulars there's a comfort to the place. Snort and Billy there tonight, sure. Shirley as snack bar counter clerk, referee. And there's Jim, now more then ever. He'd been fired from IBM and had grown a goatee and gotten an ear ring and his verbal inflections were growing more and more Mullet Luv even though he was from New Jersey. And Waymon, the center of attention more than ever. Every Wednesday night the clamor about his Masters volunteer Bermuda grass grab-and-hold not dying down, fading away, but getting worse. Waymon more than ever a curiosity. His face and Bermuda grass-cupping hand on the cover of seventy-two different golf magazines and they're scattered on the big round table. Always being held up, pointed at, shaken in Waymon's face. Bermuda grass fuckin' grabber, man. They'd worn out the snack bar VCR playing the moment of Waymon's grabbing on CBS over and over.

Tonight Waymon was, like it or not, "The Unexplained." Sweat drying, he'd hit two big baskets. Some balls solid. Some not quite right and he was scared. The Unexplained, picking at the corner of a business card he'd pulled off of the bulletin board coated with the cards of real estate agents and chiropractors. LaJuanita had a few up there. Hers noted her experience in creating award-winning Senior Prom mullets, Prison mullets, Probation mullets, Court Appearance mullets, Bass Tournament mullets, and Softball, Wedding, Divorce Court, Body Builder, NASCAR Race Weekend, and Biker mullets and that she's just introduced to America a new six-hundred-dollar hairdo for women called the "Corn Cob."

THE UNEXPLAINED: "This fella here says he can improve your game in ten swangs. Angus O'Riley. Just *ten*? Now ain't *that* something."

SHIRLEY, from behind the counter: "Sugar, he come in here the other night. I sorta felt sorry for him, so I let him put his card up there. He's a little *diff*-ernt than most of them others what I let put their cards up there."

BILLY: "If he's diff-ernt, then him and The Unexplained outta get along just *fine!*"

SNORT AND BILLY, high fives. Adam's apple-bobbing gulps of beer. Fresh cigarettes lit with squinting eyes.

Different. A little different? Waymon wore his expressions on his sleeve.

SNORT: "*Unexplaaaaaained*, the dude's goddamn fuckin' *blind*."

THE UNEXPLAINED: "That's *crazy*. How could a man teach a golf lesson if he was *blind?*"

SNORT: "And the dude hobbles around like a goddamn goat, *too*. I *seen* him, didn't I Shirley? I seen him come hobblin' in here with his goddamn cane and like he could see he trucked on over there and fuckin' tacked his card on the board and boogied his gimp ass right on *outta* here! It was goddamn *weird*. I shot him a *bird*."

SHIRLEY, distastefully: "Sure, *Snort*, you *seen* him. You was sittin' right there in a puddle of your own juices. So *what* you shot him a bird?" Shirley rolled her eyes. Drunk speak. Every so often it made sense, but not tonight.

SNORT, distastefully, as he banged his empty beer can on the table: "Bring me another goddamn Miller Lite, woman."

BILLY: "Yeah, me goddamn, *too. Me* want one."

JIM, looking real Mullet Luv now with that new goatee and the subtle beginnings of the local hairdo and a hard pot belly, born of robotic, nightly beer drinking with Snort and Billy at the Mullet Luv Golf Center: "Yeah, baby. I'm horny for one, *too*."

SHIRLEY: "God, you dumb country hick redneck sister marryers."

Waymon called the blind man when he got home and met him on the range the next night after a session of fornication. She skipped the boob-soaping-up part as they were getting tender after so much recent action. Waymon had skinny hands but they were strong.

A blind golf instructor. Waymon chuckled to himself. What the heck. And the blind shall see. Asked me did my clubs fit, like my shoes. Didn't teach people whose clubs don't fit.

A taxi brought him. He hobbled like a goat and used a cane and was blind. He brought a stool, a green Masters stool with the logo (another omen), and sat down next to Waymon's big basket. Not a word while Waymon took warm-up swings. He was listening to them. Then he asked for twenty dollars.

Waymon gave him the money but he never put it in his pocket, just held it in his hand.

From a passing pickup truck, someone yelled, "Five, ass-*hoooole!*"

Waymon didn't look. Eyes on the teacher there, sitting on the Masters stool.

"Ten balls," the man said. "Ten only."

"Okay. Mr. O'Riley, what club should I use?"

"An iron."

"Which one?"

"A *five.*"

Waymon already had it in his hand. Couldn't believe he was doing this. Knew how stupid he'd look if he told the man his goal was to shoot a sixty-two at Augusta National Golf Club.

Snort and Billy and Jim, down a few stations, making faces, belching, whacking. Beers drunk in two gulps then cans pressed into the forehead. Basketball shots with the pressed cans at the mesh trash baskets. Air cans.

Waymon: "Ready?"

He nodded.

Waymon hit.

"On the *toe.*"

"Yeah, it was." Waymon looked at the clubface. A white smudge with stretched out dimple marks, like gaping, screaming mouths.

"Why?"

"I'm just swanging at it. I'm not trying to hit it solid."

He shrugged his shoulders.

Waymon hit number two solid. The third on the toe again.

"You *swung* too fast."

"I did."

"Then don't *swing* fast. Seven away from knowing everything."

Number four: fairly solid.

"Not quite?"

"No, sir."

"Why?"

"*You* know why. Next ball."

Number five: topped it.

"Why'd you *top* it?"

"This is making me nervous."

"What part scares you the most? You've never taken golf lessons from an old blind man?"

"It's knowing how to hit a golf ball perfectly but not doing it."

"You're not scared, you're lazy. It takes about two and a half seconds to hit a golf shot perfectly. Two and a half seconds, son."

"I'm not a lazy person. I'm really not."

"Then hit five perfect shots in a row, Waymon Poodle. I *dare* you."

State Ammo

Six weeks later Waymon Poodle won the Georgia State Men's Amateur Championship at East Lake Golf Club.

Waymon won it all right.

He did.

The Atlanta newspaper shouted his story in "Sports," then the next Sunday in "Living," on the front page with a big color photo of his face.

Who? *Who* won our prestigious state amateur championship?

The *bank* teller.

Who?

The guy who plays out of that shit wad Mullet Luv Golf Center. You ever gone up there and played that toilet? Rednecks in coach's shorts. Brains and shirts and shoes are *not* required. I been up there man, and it's scary.

The *weird* looking guy?

You know, the Masters volunteer guy. He was on the cover of every goddamn golf magazine grabbing that woman's Bermuda grass. And on goddamn CBS.

Oh *that* guy. Yeah, he's an American *hero!*

Waymon won it all right.

By five shots.

Toby?

Because Waymon felt guilty about beating all those other nice fellows in the state amateur—the first golf tournament he'd ever played in—and then watched as forty-two of them, who looked as if they'd been preparing their entire lives to win this one single event, wept in the parking lot, he felt he should punish himself.

So he turned his computer on, pulled up the Internet, and typed in that certain address, then hit Search. Shakily, wearily, and with extreme tension.

PROFESSOR JEEVPIL BISWAPATI'S ULTIMATE!
AND EXCLUSIVE!
GIANT CICADA KILLER WASP WEB SITE

....

http://www.georgiainstituteoftechnology.edu/Entomology/~biswapati/KILLER.html

....

September 2007

They have not found Toby.

A new employee, Toby had not yet had his Augusta National Golf Club Employee Location Microchip surgically inserted under his scalp. They have a big electronic "course layout" on the wall in a place at Augusta National Golf Club called the center of golf course maintenance used to monitor the activities of these tobacco spitters and their machinery. This is one sophisticated place, my devotees.

Cuddled in the arms of the mukhya nyayadhish, I tell them, Toby is. They do not know who the hell the mukhya nyayadhish is. Or Toby is still barely alive and most likely being "cocooned" by the super whoppers in their underground burrow, the super whoppers slowly sucking out Toby's juices like in "Aliens" (see photo below courtesy of Warner Bros.).

Mukhya nyayadhish help me. I have decided to take on this super whopper elimination process myself. I am used to delegating to under-classmen as you know, but now I must, as they say in sports vernacular, "step up." The flame-thrower has arrived. It is a goddamn fire-breathing dragon. In the get-to-know-each-other phase, I have already killed two bulldozers, what they call a "flag" "stick," melted my long fingernails, and singed the tip of my jibh.

From far away, my devotees, I have spied the super whoppers with a pair of really powerful binoculars. And they have spied me. They wait for me at this place called the twelfth tee. I have been told by the locals and the tobacco spitters that the thang is a "par three," the toughest par three in the world of championship golfing competition.

But this is no championship competition like you enjoy in your pansy-ass intramural volleyball games with your cold beers and gurgling hookah bongs and your bisexual girlfriends and your infected tattoos and eyelid rings when you should be studying about giant cicada killer wasps. This is a fight to the death. If I survive, you will find me at Hooters, cuddled in the arms of Pam.

My devotees, I will tell you this so listen the hell up. Main vahan ja raha hun!

■   ■   ■

Waymon's Reaction to
Professor Biswapati's Latest News

Talking to his computer screen in the eerie quiet of apartment 1931:
"Lord, I don't *want* to skip the twelfth *hole*. That's where
I want to make a *bir*die. Now I've been telling you
that for *years—dang it.*"

PART VI

A Dream Come Blue

Butler Cabin Fever

As irritating as it was to people, especially to those foreign people who bag groceries and always stare at Waymon, even while they're bagging groceries, and even when they're mopping up something they spilled because they dropped something onto the floor while they were busy staring at Waymon when they should have been watching what they were bagging, Waymon was bright and cheerful on Monday mornings when he got to work. God forbid they knew he was bright and cheerful before he got to work.

Waymon never had to worry about a Monday morning hangover, and since he was the last to leave the branch on Saturday afternoon, he gladly finished up the last business and turned off the lights and the copier and the coffee machine and locked the door, so the slate was clean and ready for action come Monday morning, and that made Waymon happy as he loved his job so much. Sometimes on Saturday afternoons Waymon might be all the way in the parking lot, about to stick the key into the lock of his Diplomat, and then all of a sudden run back and unlock the branch door and check the contents of the employee refrigerator just to make sure that something turning to goo or spewing mold got thrown away.

On the Monday morning of the week Waymon was to play Augusta National Golf Club, there he sat, serving a multitude of valuable customers.

Very badly.

Which was unlike Waymon Poodle, the friendliest, most competent of any teller in any branch in all five states and the District of Columbia in which TrustTrust did business. He really shouldn't have been distracted and irritable. That summer he won the state amateur championship, just like Bob Jones did once, the founder of Augusta National Golf Club. Waymon's game was in perfect shape for the practice range and that big practice green they have and the sloping fairways and slick greens of Augusta National Golf Club.

It was just that he didn't know yet what the plan was. Waymon liked to know what the plans were. The president of TrustTrust or that crazy Mr. Dilworth fellow or the Augusta National Golf Club head pro or that crazy

Betty Simpson, if she still works there, hadn't called him yet. So Waymon was distracted and irritable. He was desperately thinking about why the phone wasn't ringing or why he hadn't got a FedEx delivery from Augusta National Golf Club or why the phone wasn't ringing or—

Just then, the phone rang.

Waymon wondered if the omens were still coming even though he was set, or supposed to be. A moment later, instead of with a perceptible level of obnoxia, but with an extreme level of obnoxia, Waymon called from the break room for Waymon to come get the phone.

Waymon trotted back there. Waymon grabbed for the phone, but Waymon jerked it back before he could get it. Waymon said, "It's your *golf* buddy, the president of TrustTrust Banks. Hoo-dee-*doo*."

"That's not nice, saying hoo-dee-*doo* like that. Give me that *phone*." Waymon grabbed for the phone again.

"I've been working at TrustTrust for twenty-three *years* and I ain't *never* talked to the president. And here's ol' Waymon Poodle just yakking it up with him. So, hoo-dee-doo-*doo*."

Waymon grabbed the phone and bumped Waymon out of the chair and sat down. "Now that I *really* don't like. Adding *doo*-doo to it."

"Then how about hoo-dee-*shit*-shit."

Waymon's eyes widened. "Now that's just downright sacrilegious, and dang *foul*-mouthed."

"Hoo-dee-*shit*-shit, then."

Now Waymon's mouth hung open. His eyes were still wide, too.

Waymon pointed a finger at Waymon. "So what do ya think about *that*, you Bible thumper!"

"I'm a Bible reader!" Waymon pointed for Waymon to go up to the front and sort of wiggled his finger for Waymon to shut the door, too.

The moment Waymon got up to the front he hit the buzzer. *Buzz… buzzzz.*

Waymon sucked in a huge breath and then stuck the phone to the side of his face. "Sir, Waymon *Poodle* here. I can't tell you how exci—"

"*Waymon*," the president said in a chilling tone, "I have some rather bad *news* to deliver. Rather, well, bad… as *hell*."

Waymon scrunched his face up. "It's not about Saturday is it?" Waymon's heart was already racing. He cupped the phone and took another huge breath and began reciting the Lord's Prayer in his mind.

"*Well*, son. It's about Saturday *and* Friday."

Nothing.

Buzz… buzz… buzz.

"What's that goddamn *buzzing* noise? You there, Waymon?"

"Yessir. What do you mean 'Friday?'"

"Well, I'm just afraid you might not like how I've mangled this whole thing *up*. You being so deserving to play golf at Augusta National Golf Club."

Resolved to it now. Never, ever question God's design. The fornication with that horny dang LaJuanita. Soaping up all her boobs. Waymon began to weep.

The president said, "I just hate that you'll have to come down Friday afternoon instead of Saturday morning and stay in the Butler Cabin with me and Dilworth here and Jack *Nick*-lawse."

Nothing again. Waymon's expression like the moment of the revealing of the Bermuda grass. As if he'd seen a ghost. He didn't like it when people pronounced Mr. Nicklaus' name like that. But maybe that really was the way to do it. Now Waymon wasn't exactly sure. Now Waymon was real confused.

Buzzzzzz.

"Waymon, I keep losing you here. I'm a busy man doing things."

"Sir, I'm—did you say Jack Ni—"

"See, I'm just afraid you might not like to get on down to the ol' *golf* club on Friday afternoon and get settled in the ol' Butler Cabin, you know where they do part of the ol' TV thing down there, and have dinner with Jack and me and *Dil*worth. I'll show you our wine cellar."

"Sir, I'm—did you say Jack Ni—"

"*Right.* Now I got elected Membership Committee Chairman this summer and for God knows why the Entomology Committee Chairman and at dinner with Jack on Friday night I'm going to tell him he's been elected to the membership since he might have been miffed we let Ed Fiori in a couple of years ago so that moment will be a hugely historic moment in the history of golf and you'll be right there at the dinner table with him when I give him the good news. To get him to come we told him we were going to pay him ten million dollars to redesign a bunker and he cleared his schedule for two days. Hey, Waymon, you know they call Jack Nick-lawse the Golden *Bear?*"

Snickering heard in the background of the president's office.

Buzz… buzzzzz.

Waymon staring off into space. Mouth gaping. Tears of joy now. As we forgive those who trespass against us…

"And then Saturday morning we'll pack our bellies with a monstrously greasy breakfast and burp real loud and then tee it up with Jack. *Jack,* baby, Waymon. First tee time. First day of the season. You know you measly guests can't play from the tournament tees—we got this big rule that says measly guests can't play from the tournament tees—but guess what I finagled. Just *guess.* I really hope that sounds okay. I just hope I haven't mangled this thing up for you, Waymon." The president burped real loud.

Waymon wiped his cheek with the back of his hand. "No, sir. Of *course* not. Praise Jeesus."

"Yeah, okay, *Jesus,* sure. *Hey,* so bring a coat and tie for Friday night. You got a green jacket, Waymon?" The president wanted to laugh so badly but he thought he might burst an artery. Got a green jacket.

Dilworth snickering so hard he's about to pee in his pants. Both hands pressed over his mouth. Red-faced, beating his shoes on the carpet as if he were stomping fire ants. And so goddamn happy he got invited. Had to kiss ass and lick crack and wipe crack and brown nose and suck up every day, all summer long. And beg. He was exhausted.

The president rolling his eyes. "Waymon? You there?"

"Here, sir," Waymon said meekly, wet faced.

"And *hey,* congratulations on that state am, Waymon. Aren't *you* the total package?"

T.G.I.T.

Thursday.

Because Waymon never got a transaction right all week, pretty much beginning Monday morning, Waymon fired him on Thursday afternoon.

Waymon waited for everybody to leave and as Waymon was pouring the tar-like goo substance of the office coffee into the sink, Waymon up and fired him.

Waymon turned around and gave Waymon a strange look. He didn't say anything at first, just like when LaJuanita hit him with the fornication ultimatum, so Waymon chewed on the situation for a moment. Surely, the last thing in the world Waymon Poodle would be accused of was being pompous or arrogant. But Waymon really did have a relationship with the president of the whole dang company. He thought at that moment, here was a man who was a member of Augusta National Golf Club, the same gentleman who invited me to meet him at Augusta National Golf Club less than twenty-four hours from this moment to play golf and hang out with him and Jack Nicklaus at Augusta National Golf Club. So if Waymon had ever done the same thing with the president of Trust Trust Banks and Jack Nicklaus at Augusta National Golf Club, he would have made a big deal out of it for a month. This was a heady feeling for Waymon. Waymon said, with a slight bit of pomposity in his voice, "I don't think you can *fire* me."

Waymon waggled a finger at Waymon. "Oh, yes I *can!*"

Waymon had what are called "donkey smarts," and knew that when dealing with people such as Waymon who he felt like didn't have donkey smarts, not one bit, it was best to just agree to whatever it was they wanted then shut your mouth. Use your donkey smarts. Call their bluff. So Waymon said, using his donkey smarts, "Okay then." And walked out.

"*Hey!*" Waymon yelled. "You can't walk out like that! I just *fired* you!"

Bunkered Up

Waymon Poodle had the heebie-jeebies real bad.

Friday morning real early he was rolling around on the grass in front of his apartment as if he were on fire. Actually, it wasn't grass Waymon was rolling around on. It was more like hard packed red dirt with a few small rocks and bullet casings and bits of concrete blocks and clumps of hair with the skin still attached and a whole bunch of beer caps and an eyeball that kept getting pressed into his shirt and his kneecaps and some old cigarette butts were getting stuck in his hair too.

Mr. Gable, of course, was watching this scene from afar with his Chihuahua and didn't see Waymon with a pistol in his hand with a silencer on it, or a rifle with a scope with a silencer on it, or a knife in his hand, or a sharp ice pick in his hand so he walked over to Waymon and asked him what the fuck he was doing.

While he was still rolling around on the dirt, Waymon said, "I don't want these new… *golf* clothes… I bought last night at *Dillard's*… to look too new. You know?"

"Not really," Mr. Gable said.

Waymon stood up and brushed himself off. There was a cigarette butt in his ear. "I just think I'll look like a hick if my golf clothes look too new when I pass through the holy *gates* this afternoon."

"Waymon?"

"Yessir. Mr. Gable?"

That Chihuahua barked specifically at Waymon then started gnawing on a flea on his leg.

"Can I tell you something that's been on my mind for a long time and you not get all fuckin' messed up?"

"Well, *sure*, Mr. Gable."

"Waymon, you've got to be the strangest cat I've ever met in my life. And I've known shit loads of strange and dangerous cats." Mr. Gable squinted at Waymon. "But I love you, Waymon. You really are a dangerous fuckin' country hick. A real perfect example. Like they use in the movies. You know what I mean?"

"No."

So Waymon went back inside and put his dirty golf clothes in the washer—cold, one rinse, delicate—and while his clothes were getting washed he called Waymon at the bank branch to make sure if he really was fired or not, just to make sure. To think that he could have served some valuable customers from his bank branch window on the very same day he'd pass through the gate of Augusta National Golf Club, even though he'd have to leave work earlier than normal, delighted Waymon quite a lot.

"What part of 'You're fired' don't you understand, *Waymon?*" Waymon said real mean.

Waymon thought his heebie-jeebies might let up once he got on the road and started listening to gospel music, but they didn't. He didn't want to drive too fast because he didn't want to get a ticket, but he got a ticket near Siloam on I-20 anyway because he was driving too slow.

Waymon honestly thought that all those people riding up on his tail in the left lane, then swerving around him and honking their horns and making arm and hand and ferocious facial gestures, knew, somehow, that he was traveling to Augusta National Golf Club to play golf. Waymon honestly thought that those who are about to play Augusta National Golf Club had an aura and that it was real obvious. Even their cars.

Waymon took a right onto Berckmans Road and went down there to see if they had come and gotten the twelfth green, and it looked like they had, so he drove to the holy gates and stopped the Diplomat, which was hissing like a cat and steaming like a volcano, by the guard house. Waymon could not have cared less about his car about to blow up. He glanced over his shoulder to the back seat to make sure his golf clubs and his golf shoes were still back there and they were, and this made him feel very nice. Not that they would have gone anywhere. This was just the kind of thing heebie-jeebies made Waymon do six hundred and four times, smiling oddly, during the drive down I-20 to Augusta in the left hand lane going real slow.

As he had hoped an enormous number of times in his life, Waymon's name was on a list with the guard in the guardhouse on Washington Road. So Waymon drove through the gate after the guard saluted and told him how nice it was to have him as a guest and hopefully many, many times in the future. Waymon said under his breath, "Lord God Jesus, thank you very much." The guard scribbled down Waymon's tag number as he drove away.

Waymon, then, with the Lord God Jesus' assistance since his hands were shaking so violently, drove slowly, reverently, desperately trying not to run over all those weird-looking magnolia pine cone things on the asphalt of Magnolia Lane, even though at the time there weren't any weird-looking magnolia pine cone things on the asphalt of Magnolia Lane. But if there were, Waymon would not have run over them.

He did not go and have lunch in the men's grill, into the pro shop to say hello and thank them and to buy seventeen logoed shirts, onto the practice range, then onto the first tee of Tea Olive, however. Or to see that dang Betty Simpson.

He parked in front of the Butler Cabin and was immediately met by an ancient man in a white waiter-style jacket and a white shirt and black tie who took his suitcase and walked inside with it and took it to Waymon's room and unpacked it and saw a need to begin ironing his golf shirt and a pair of pants and was planning to steam this fellow's bright orange jacket as it had been crammed in there too. Waymon graduated from Clemson a year early and the orange jacket was a gift from his six different grateful, exhausted guidance counselors. It was the only sport jacket he had ever owned and Waymon thought it really made him stand out when he wore it to special occasions although this was Waymon's first special occasion in his life.

Waymon took a deep breath and blew it out as he stood in the living room. Even this gave him the heebie-jeebies, as he thought that taking a deep breath and blowing it out at Augusta National Golf Club, like those erections he had during the Masters, would be rude and sacrilegious. Just then a bedroom door opened and a blond-haired man, shorter than Waymon, walked up to Waymon in only a pair of white grippies and a little pot belly and introduced himself. "Hi there, Jack Nick-lawse."

Waymon didn't—couldn't—say anything for a moment. He just held his right hand out. Jack Nicklaus grabbed it. "Son, you got a *name?* You look like you'd have a *good* one."

"Nick-lawse?"

"No that's *my* name."

"*Poodle.* Waymon Poodle from Mullet Luv, Georgia."

"Well then, it's real nice to meet you, Waymon. You're playing golf here tomorrow?"

"Yessir. With you and two other gentlemen. I'm so exci—"

"Oh, no. I'd *like* to, because I really love to play golf, but the Golden Bear is here to look at redesigning a bunker. Ten million for it, but if that's what they want to pay the Golden Bear, dang let them. Know what I *mean?*"

Waymon said, zombie-like, "You're the greatest golfer in the *world*."

"Well, that's what they say. Hey, the Golden Bear is hungry. You wanna go chow down?"

So Waymon Poodle went and put on his bright orange jacket and the Golden Bear put on his green jacket and they walked to the clubhouse together. Waymon had prepared two hundred and sixty-two questions for the Golden Bear, but he found that his throat had closed up and he couldn't speak. Waymon looked off to his left and saw a hot air balloon hovering over where the par three twelfth would be and thought it was a pleasant scene. Just then, from way down there, it looked as if someone poked a nice campfire and made it flame up for a second, but Waymon wasn't sure. Maybe the members had campfires and hot air balloon races out here when they had the club to themselves, Waymon thought. Could be. Who knows? Waymon had so deeply suppressed into the particular lobe of his brain that deals with this sort of thing, the knowledge of a particular Hindu entomologist who recently acquired a flame thrower and was using the flame thrower to fry a super whopper giant cicada killer wasp down around the twelfth tee at Augusta National Golf Club, that it didn't occur to Waymon at that moment what the "flame up" really was. Just so deeply suppressed.

The Golden Bear, as they walked near the practice putting green, could tell that they had moved the practice putting green two feet and three inches to the left.

As they walked into the clubhouse, Waymon's heebie-jeebies subsided just a little as he discovered he hadn't thought about super whopper giant cicada killer wasps one bit as they were walking unprotected across the grounds. But then, as soon as he thought about not thinking about them, he immediately started thinking about them, and his heebie-jeebies came back to the level they were a few minutes ago.

Waymon and the Golden Bear walked into the dining room and saw that the president of TrustTrust and Dilworth were already sitting at a table. Dilworth had the heebie-jeebies real bad, too, so he had slurped down eight scotches hoping that they would calm his heebie-jeebies down but they didn't. So he was drooling and he also had over two hundred questions for the Golden Bear.

"GENTLEMEN!" the president of TrustTrust screamed from across the room, then came jogging over. (Six pina coladas already.) "*Jack*, baby? You meet Waymon?"

"The Golden Bear met Waymon." The Golden Bear gave Waymon a pleasant look, then his face suddenly contorted. "Hey, I *knew* it. You're that fella who grabbed Betty Simpson's Bermu—"

"Nice *jacket* by the way, Waymon," the president blurted out with pina colada breath, running his fingers along a lapel. "*Damn* that thing's orange."

"Thank you, sir."

"Really, it's orange *all day*."

"*Thank* you."

"Maybe until the end of *time*, Waymon—that jacket. You hunt deer in that thing?"

Waymon gazed down at a sleeve. "Thank you so much."

The president winked and nudged the Golden Bear with a knuckle. "Hey Waymon, I thought I told you to wear your *green* jacket."

"I don't own a green jacket, sir. Just this orange one."

The president whacked Waymon on the back. "Well not yet, right Waymon? I mean you could *get* one, one day, *right*? You just come on down here again and win the goddamn Masters, by God, and we'll give you a green jacket for *free*!" The president laughed real loud, then poked a finger into the Golden Bear's belly button. "Hell, Jack, baby, you got *six*. You don't wear them all at one time, do you? So why doncha run your ass upstairs and get Waymon one?" The president cackled so loudly the dining room manager and the sommelier and a guy with a broom poked their heads out of the kitchen door.

The Golden Bear gave the president a cool look. You really don't joke around about the jacket. Takes a lot of toil and pain and suffering to get one. Heck, you nearly die getting one. And those stupid questions you have to answer afterwards. Sacrilegious, really, to joke about, even a member joking about it. Like having an erection or something while you're here. Sure, I've had erections during casual rounds and even during the Masters. Had forty-nine erections back when I was reigning United States Amateur Champion right up there in the Crow's Nest. Erections are permissible at Augusta National Golf Club under the proper circumstances, okay, but you just don't joke about the green threads.

The president whacked the Golden Bear on the back. "*Jack*, baby, you know this guy in the orange jacket might have grabbed Betty Simpson's Bermuda grass on goddamn international TV. I mean, he grabbed the *hell* outta that thing, but did you know that he's also the best teller in my whole company?"

"The Golden Bear didn't know that. Congratulations, Waymon." The Golden Bear whacked Waymon on the back.

Waymon perked up. "Sir?"

"Yes, Waymon?"

"I'm not a teller any more. I got *fired* yesterday."

"Well *hell*, you musta wore that crazy orange jacket to work. You wear that damn thing to work, Waymon?"

"No, sir. I was sort of distracted all week because—"

"*Right!*" The president whacked Waymon on the back. "Because you were thinking about playing Augusta goddamn National *Golf* Club! *That's* what! Something im*portant*. Hell, you'll probably find another job in a couple of years. So, *Jack*, baby. Waymon. Thirsty? Hungry?"

The Golden Bear looked at Waymon who looked as if he were about to faint, which he could do sometimes when the heebie-jeebies reached a critical level.

Waymon blinked a few times.

The Golden Bear whacked Waymon on the back. "It looks like we are."

After they got settled at the table the president of TrustTrust leaned down as if he were saying something real secret. Dilworth had passed out but had not fallen out of his chair. Under the table the president stabbed him with a fork where he thought Dilworth's left nut would be. Dilworth came to, but he didn't give the immediate impression that he was focused. "Fellas, listen, we got a load of nine-pound lobsters in today from Omaha or someplace. I hope you all like nine-pound lobsters?"

"The Golden Bear likes a nine-pound lobster."

"Me, too," Dilworth said like a little kid. "I *love* 'em. Nine-pound loz-baters."

The president gave Dilworth a hard look, then stabbed him in the kneecap.

A waiter appeared.

The president of TrustTrust said to the waiter, "*Flapjack*, how *big* are those nine-pound lobsters you got back there? Huh?"

Flapjack held his hands out as if showing the size of a fish. "'Bout this big."

"*Naw*, they're bigger than *that!*"

"*This* big."

"Naw, they're about the size of—the size of *what*, Flapjack?"

"Small crocodile?"

"Nine-pound lobsters, by God. That's what they look like, boys. A small crocodile." The president leaned over and nudged Waymon with a knuckle. "Waymon, you like a nine-pound lobster?"

"I've never *eaten* a lobster, sir."

"Well, you are tonight. A nine-pounder. Size of a small crocodile! Flapjack!"

"Yessir?"

"Nine-pound lobsters"—he waved his arm in a circle—"all around!"

Knowing he was going to eat a nine-pound sea creature with red claws heightened the level of Waymon's heebie-jeebies but the chardonnay they made him drink squelched some of them. The bread and the butter was real good so Waymon crammed a whole bunch of that in his mouth and listened to these men talk about matters of great importance to the wonderful world of golf and to the commerce of the global community of earth. All of a sudden, the Golden Bear asked the president what bunker it was he was going to be redesigning. "The Golden Bear thinks it's the one behind the green at five?"

"Naw, Jack, baby, the real reason we asked you—"

The nine-pound lobsters were plunked down in front of them on huge platters. Waymon's heart began to race.

"Say, that big squiggly one," the Golden Bear blurted out, "in the middle of the tenth fairway? Redesign it? Or why don't we just get *rid* of it. Nobody ever uses it anyway. Huh?"

"Naw, shut up a second."

The Golden Bear cut off a huge wad of nine-pound lobster and shoved it in.

"Now this is about to be a real historic moment in the history of golf and the private club industry, so pardon me if I'm a little formal all of a sudden. *Jack*, baby?"

"Mmmm?" He was chewing.

"Welcome to the club."

"Great to be here. I love a good lobster."

"*You* know"—the president winked and nudged him with a knuckle—"welcome to the club. Get it?"

"Really delicious."

Waymon Poodle, the chardonnay now coursing through his veins and arteries and capillaries like the Niagara, so frustrated at this wink-wink, nudge-nudge thing going on while the greatest golfer in the world was trying to enjoy his nine-pound lobster, suddenly stood up as if he'd been electrocuted, then made golf history again by being the one who told the Golden Bear they had finally made him a member of Augusta National Golf Club, so welcome. If Waymon ever had bad heebie-jeebies in his life, he really did then. So right after he delivered the wonderful news to the Golden Bear in his squawking voice, he finally fainted onto his lobster and his glass of wine and the basket of bread, then slid off the lobster onto the floor and sort of quivered for a moment and then went limp.

So it was a real memorable moment in the history of golf.

From the September 2007 issue of *Go Figure,*
the monthly report of the
American Psychological Association

———————

*We were intrigued by recent studies that prove golf really
messes male humans up real good.*

*The golfer who has finally obtained a tee time at
Augusta National Golf Club, we discovered, becomes
immediately disoriented and might brush his teeth with his
toenail clipper. The subject fails to wave "thank you" to people
who let him merge into traffic. The infants of these subjects
waddle aimlessly through their home, dragging around
six pound poo-poo diapers. These subjects, who now
frequently run out of gas, sit in the middle of an interstate
highway, dislocomoted, and don't care one bit,
even while a state patrolman taps on their window with the
tip of his .357 magnum. The golfer's tendency, who now has
this tee time, is to gaze into space and smile.*

Sunscream

In the world of golfing men, when the threesome and their loyal caddies step upon the first tee, that moment is always fraught with fresh heebie-jeebie-type emotions for all of those six people. It doesn't even necessarily matter if it's the first tee of Augusta National Golf Club or the first tee of the Mullet Luv Golf Center. That's just the way it is in the world of golfing men.

Of course, an uninformed observer of the world of golfing men would think that since these peculiar people have spent time on the practice range warming up their minds and muscles for the day ahead and have temporarily re-trained their bodies to remember what to do, then it would seem that the moment spent on the first tee, or the tenth tee if the nines had been reversed that day because of something, would be a period of utter confidence about the whole deal.

Not really the case, though, with the first group on the first tee on the first day of the season at Augusta National Golf Club.

In the feeding frenzy of the evening, Dilworth forgot, after seven pounds of lobster had been gulped down, that he was allergic to shellfish, so his head swelled up right there in front of everybody in the dining room and itchy, red blisters emerged on one hundred and three percent of his body, and that morning he and his head and his body were still being watched in his room in the Butler Cabin by a physician Augusta National Golf Club had on retainer for when guests did stupid things when they played or ate there for the first time, which was a lot.

So Dilworth was out.

The Golden Bear had hit some really great practice shots with just his telescoping ball retriever, amazing everyone, after he stretched on the ground for nearly thirty minutes and had a belly that was packed with a monstrously greasy breakfast. So he was ready to go, even though he could have gone back home since he learned he wasn't really there to re-design a bunker for ten million dollars, although the Ed Fiori thing sort of miffed him a little bit. But the Golden Bear really loved to play golf, so there he was. The Golden Bear burped real loud four times.

The president of TrustTrust, whose belly was also packed with a monstrously greasy breakfast, was still feeling guilty about Waymon just lying there under the table while they finished their nine-pound lobsters and some fabulous tiramisu. Waymon was breathing, so that was good. They kept looking down there every once and a while to check. And there wasn't anybody else in the dining room so they all agreed it was okay for him just to rest until Flapjack tripped over Waymon and nearly gouged out one of the Golden Bear's eyeballs with one of those little espresso spoons, which are fairly sharp. The president loved to play golf, too. He tried to match burps with the Golden Bear but instead gagged up part of his omelet, which he just re-swallowed to save time.

On the first tee, Waymon, whose belly was also packed with a monstrously greasy breakfast, felt as if he was from outer space. His dream had come true in more incredible ways than he'd ever imagined, and now that prosperity had arrived, and he thought he'd be joyous about it, instead he found that he was twitching. Not much, but enough for his caddie to walk over, tentatively, and give him a wet towel. Waymon didn't look like he liked to play golf or even knew how. Waymon didn't even burp real loud—even though he could have and not gotten in any trouble at Augusta National Golf Club—because he felt that burping real loud at Augusta National Golf Club, especially on the first tee of Tea Olive, was just as sacrilegious as the erection business.

As for the caddies, Waymon had indeed been assigned the best and wisest caddie at Augusta National Golf Club, just as he dreamed. The caddie was called "Albert Einstein," and he really did seem good at being a caddie and wise. In the pockets of Albert Einstein's caddie overalls were six disposable cameras from Wal-Mart that Waymon had given him. Two cameras had already been used up on the practice range with one or two of Albert Einstein's fingers in all the shots.

The Golden Bear's caddie was the one he always asked for when he came up for a casual round and that caddie was called "Birdie Train." The president of TrustTrust's caddie, even though he always wanted Birdie Train but had to give him up for the Golden Bear this time, was a new kid from the local medical college whose real name was Mike, and who went by Mike, and who was an irritating know-it-all.

Everybody perked up when the president of TrustTrust all of a sudden said: "*Now*, before we begin to play this wonderful game of *golf*, I must give you all a little warning. As Chairman of the Augusta National Golf Club Entomology Committee, which was formed real quick this spring, I feel obliged to inform you people that we have a little *wasp* problem out here at the ol' club. Anybody ever heard of a super whopper giant cicada killer wasp?"

Waymon, still having the twitches, twitched violently. The twitch looked as if he were fanning cigarette smoke away.

"So *Waymon*, you've heard of these things."

Waymon twitched violently again. This time as if he were reaching out to shake hands. Twice.

The Golden Bear moved away from him just a little bit.

"Well *good* then, because for some reason that's real hard to figure, we've had an infestation of these fascinating creatures. And I'm sorry to say that it's a particularly fascinating mutate form of these bugs called super whopper giant cicada killer wasps, and although our special super whopper giant cicada killer wasp on-site consultant tells me we're down to *one* now, and he's real *nasty*, they've indeed caused havoc and mayhem here at the ol' club. May we have a brief moment of silence for a maintenance employee named Toby."

They had a brief moment of silence for Toby.

"Now the last one of these things has been observed to be holding fort at the tee box of Golden Bell and although I don't think we'll have to *skip* that hole—"

Waymon finally began to smile.

"—I just feel that I'm pretty much off the hook *legally* since I informed you people of this pesky menace thing. Thus endeth my prepared remarks."

That caddie Mike rolled his eyes.

Albert Einstein silently prayed that he wouldn't have to tangle with a mutate damn wasp because he had a date tonight with a nasty, freak bitch with long, curled-up fingernails.

Birdie Train sucked on a cigarette as he adjusted the position of his enormous testicles merely by subtly shifting his weight. He learned the technique from Phil Blackmar in 1988 or maybe it was 1989 when they were in that playoff.

The Golden Bear gazed lovingly at the gallon milk jug-sized head of his brand new, never-before-tested, what-would-be-retail-priced-at $8,700,

Japanese-made prototype driver called "The Lincoln Continental." The Japanese promised the Golden Bear he could hit a drive with this thing—even on the hosel or the ferrule—that would go four hundred and twenty-three yards with a pleasant fade and that he'd never chicken-hook again. That's what the Japanese told him, and then a bunch of them had bowed, and then he designed a course for them.

"So everybody feels that they've been legally notified?"

Nobody really said anything except for Mike. He looked around at everybody and finally said, "Mister, see—"

"Son, my name's not 'Mister.'"

"Well, whatever your *name* is, I really don't think just blabbing about this mutate wasp situation will stand up. See, mister, my father's a big fat lawyer and if somebody'll give me their cell phone I'll call him to check because I really don't think just bla—"

"Mike... *Mike*," the president of TrustTrust growled.

"Shit! *What?*" Mike said.

"Pinch my weenie. Everybody?"

Pleasant, expectant expressions all around, except for Mike's.

"Game on."

Waymon eagled the first hole with a nice approach shot with an 8-iron so he was feeling a whole lot better even though he would have been enormously pleased with a birdie or a routine par or a tap in for bogey.

"Go easy on the Golden Bear, Waymon," the Golden Bear said to Waymon as they walked to the second tee, which took them a while since it had been moved, this time forward by one hundred and fourteen yards and a quarter.

At the turn, Waymon was six under and the Golden Bear was not, so the Golden Bear was now mildly irritated. In kind of a sweet fatherly way, sure, but still irritated that this cross-eyed cat was whipping him. Then when the Golden Bear finally asked Waymon how he became so good at golfing Waymon told him that the fellow who'd been giving him lessons all summer really had to get a lot of the credit, even though he was blind. So that bit of information just made the Golden Bear even more mildly irritated and therefore he chicken-hooked it at ten. He'd never chicken-hooked in his life unless he was trying to. The Golden Bear gawked at the head of The Lincoln Continental as if the details on why he chicken-hooked were printed on the face of the club.

The president of TrustTrust forgot to wipe the sunscreen off of his hands so now all that shit was on his grips and he was not having a good season opener at all.

Dilworth, still laid out in the Butler Cabin, was continuing to not have a good season opener at all either.

The Ascension

When some guy is winning at golf more than the rest of the guys in his group, this situation has a habit of infecting the way he walks.

Most guys who are winning at golf walk as if they've had the scorecard pencil carefully placed between their butt cheeks and they walk in a quick-step, confident, from-point-A-to-point-B sort of way as if they're actually trying to keep the scorecard pencil from falling out and this way of walking is real irritating to those who have noticed and are not winning.

This was the way Waymon was walking to the twelfth tee after making a lip-out par on the eleventh as opposed to another person's double bogey in the pond (the Golden Bear) and another person's pick-up all the way back in the fairway (the president of TrustTrust).

But all was still good. The temperature of the air. Just a few cotton-white clouds that didn't threaten anything but continued meteorological aesthetic pleasure for those type of people who noticed and cared about that sort of thing. Like Waymon. Except that hot air balloon didn't quite fit in to the aesthetic pleasure situation at all.

Sure, it was one of those crisp October days, perfect for hot air bal-looning, but Waymon wondered why it had to be hovering so low in front of the green of Golden Bell, right where the ball would go. Waymon gave one of those quick glances at the president of TrustTrust as if to say, Why aren't you doing something about this, you know, sir, since you're a member of the club and a committee chairman and all?

The president, whose raw nerves could have sensed a dogwood petal falling onto the wooden bench way over at the fourth tee, was immediately irritated even more at Waymon for giving him such a snotty look but was also irritated at why a hot air balloon was right where the ball would go. If they were in trouble, then float the thing down—fine—then wad up the balloon and get the hell outta here. We're playing golf. You're where the ball would go.

The Golden Bear said, "Hello, Milt."

Milt waved back. The photographer up there in the basket with Milt, who had sixteen cameras hanging off of his neck, waved back too.

The president asked who in the hell was Milt.

"Oh, Milt *Limp*. The investigative golf journalist from the New Jersey *Oppressor*. He's real pesky."

"Well, why don't you tell him to a-*scend* if he doesn't mind? There's nothing to investigate here at Golden Bell so just go over and investigate something over there at Augusta Country Club. Everything *here* is under control." Then he said real quiet under his breath, "I *hope*."

"Milt?" the Golden Bear said.

"Yes, Mister Nick-lawse?"

"Mind ascending? We're—" then the Golden Bear made a series of intricate arm, hand and facial gestures that golfers and investigative golf journalists universally recognize as the series of intricate arm, hand and facial gestures that mean we're about to hit our golf balls if you don't mind because you're where the ball would go.

Just then Milt yanked on a cord and the hot air balloon air heater contraption made a loud noise that scared everybody to death, and even woke up Professor Biswapati who was sleeping behind the base of an enormous loblolly pine tree on the other side of the twelfth tee. Professor Biswapati fell over onto his flame thrower which was still fairly hot from an earlier shot at what he thought was that last super whopper but it was just a yellow-billed nuthatch. Which he obliterated. When the side of his face and part of his beard hit the metal he shrieked in Hindi, "Jee-sus!"

"So, gentlemen," Waymon said, not too genuinely. "Are we playing golf or not?"

"Sure, Waymon," the president said, making a horrible and rude face at Waymon. "We're playing a form of golf."

From the September 2007 issue of *Go Figure,*
the monthly report of the
American Psychological Association

———————

And there's one other thing.

*Now that the golfer is on the property of Augusta
National Golf Club to exercise this tee time he's obtained,
we have discovered that a period of intense unreality
begins and sometimes might not end, even after the golfer
blows out of the front gate and back into the Real World.*

*This unreality, our research produced, can include
an overwhelming feeling of what's called "heebie-jeebies,"
hallucinatory activity, and the possibility of actually beating
Jack Nicklaus in golf. And a bunch of other stuff.*

*Therefore, we finally conclude, that those who have played
Augusta National Golf Club, as compared to those who
have not played Augusta National Golf Club, are distinctly
different from those who almost played
Augusta National Golf Club.*

Thousands of Eyes

Albert Einstein, just as Waymon had predicted, who had complimented Waymon on his swing—every single one of them, even his putting strokes and practice swings—and never once seemed to mind that he was asked to take a picture of Waymon and his golf bag on every tee and by every green as well as when Waymon insisted he pause in front of a number of land-scaped areas and clumps of azalea bushes that were particularly memorable, leaned down and whispered in Waymon's ear, "Be cooool, now, mistah Poodle. Stay in the zone. Don't think about them mutate bugs even though this is they crib, Mistah Poodle, right *hee*-yuh." Albert Einstein was suddenly struck at the faraway expression on Waymon's face. Albert Einstein stepped back about twenty feet.

Oh, Lord God Jesus, Waymon was thinking, how incredible it was to be finally walking on the other side of the ropes and six under as he stood on the twelfth tee at Augusta National Golf Club... remember to look at the top of the pine trees behind the green... and thank you Lord God Jesus for cleaning up all the trash and half-chewed-up pieces of pimiento cheese sandwiches people spit onto the grass and the TV cameras and those awful TV tower things and the concession tents. Waymon knew that the caddie would, by that time, instinctively know his game, and Albert Einstein did, instinctively. He knew that by that time the caddie would know exactly what club to give him as he, Waymon Poodle of Mullet Luv, Georgia, stood there looking at the flag on the historic twelfth green, flapping lazily, with his right arm extended toward the caddie and his ball freshly rubbed with a wet towel and his white tee—one of a handful of them grabbed out of a wicker basket in the pro shop—shining so brightly in the sun. He knew that when he nestled his 6-iron behind the ball, something wonderful would happen: a little butterfly twittered around the ball, then lighted upon the ball. A butterfly. A little yellow one, innocent, never in harm's way as he sat on the golf ball of Waymon Poodle. Waymon watched the butterfly open and close its wings as it sat on the ball, Waymon's favorite type of golf ball, a Titleist balata 90 compression. Waymon loved the way the black Titleist lettering and the red number looked on the ball, so dang professional. He knew at that instant how he would explain the greatest moment of his life to his friends he played golf with. He would explain it in rich, somber detail. He might even tear up. Using his 6-iron as a support, Waymon leaned down to gently brush the butterfly away so he wouldn't kill it at impact, and reached out with his gloved left hand (FootJoy, light blue this time, medium) and…

"*Waymon*," the president said real quick, "as Chairman of the Augusta National Golf Club Entomology Committee, I think it's best that you don't *mess* with that thing."

The zone speaking. Waymon still leaning down, his face eight inches from the hymenoptera. "But it's just a little yellow butterfly."

Albert Einstein looked at Mike who was looking at the Golden Bear who was looking at Birdie Train who was looking at the president of TrustTrust. Then Mike looked at Birdie Train.

Black and yellow pulsating thorax. With a stinger.

"*Noooo*, mistah Poodle. You *voo*doo tawkin," Albert Einstein moaned, slipping a camera out of his pocket and up to his eye.

"*Nice* butterfly, just as I've dreamed my whooooole *life*," Waymon whispered as he stroked its wing. "Bea*uuuuutifuuuuul*."

The Golden Bear grabbed The Lincoln Continental out of his golf bag.

Birdie Train went wide-eyed. "*Naw*-suh, Mistah Nick-lawse. You need the seven. It's a seven all *day*."

"Nice little yellow butterfly at Augusta National Golf Club…"

"Waymon, *really*. As chairman of the Ento—"

The last of Feckle's beasts suddenly rose up and attached itself to the face of the Chairman of the Entomology Committee of Augusta National Golf Club, whereat he immediately went stiff and screamed, "HOLY LORD IN HEAVEN HAVE MERCY SWEET PRECIOUS JESUS!" which echoed through the pines like thousands of Augusta National Golf Club screams before him.

"*This* is attractive," Mike said.

"Oh, *Lordy*," Birdie Train said.

"Oh, Lordy, *Lordy*," Albert Einstein said.

"You got *that* right," Birdie Train said.

"You *know* I got that right," Albert Einstein said to Birdie Train, then touched knuckles with him.

"A real member's bounce," the Golden Bear said, head cocked a little as if he were reading a difficult putt.

"Sir," Waymon said in a faraway tone, "gently nudge him with the tip of your finger and he'll flutter off. And then we'll play Golden Bell together. Nice butterf—"

"Goddammit, *you* gently nudge him with the tip of your—"

So Waymon walked over and gently nudged the super whopper with the end of the grip of his 6-iron instead of the tip of his finger.

The super whopper turned around and looked at Waymon. Waymon was looking right back at it, then all of a sudden discovered what a fool he'd been. This wasn't a little yellow butterfly not one bit. It was a super whopper giant cicada killer wasp, exactly one of those creatures mentioned on that weird web site. He'd been in denial. And consumed with desire. This was what denial felt like, coupled with consuming desire. Waymon Poodle in pure denial, consumed with desire, and had heebie-jeebies real bad, with hallucinations. Waymon all of a sudden burped real loud.

The super whopper turned and looked at the president again, hissed, as only the mutate form of these wasps could do, then jumped off his face and onto the rifle shaft (s-flex, low torque) of Waymon's club. It started creeping up the shaft.

"*Waymon*," the Golden Bear said, "What club have you got?"

"The six!"

"Listen, Waymon, just drop it and hit an easy five. Or pull the seven and we'll hit it *hard*. I'll show you how to hit a hard seven. So let the *bug*"—the Golden Bear said in a rising tone of panic—"you know, have your *club*."

Waymon, frozen, gawking. Creeping over Waymon's hand now, the mutate, up his forearm, then his bicep…

Mike said, "Somebody tell me what's wrong with *this* picture."

The president said, "A golf tip on how to hit a hard seven iron from the Golden Bear, Waymon, at no less, Augusta National Golf Club, right here on historic Golden Bear—I mean Golden Bell. Oh, boy—be a real life memory." The president rolled his eyes so hard it hurt.

…and crept up Waymon's neck and over his Adam's apple and over his chin, then his quivering lips and onto Waymon's face at Augusta National Golf Club on the first day of the season on Golden Bell, tournament tees, one hundred and fifty-five yards with a slight right to right to left, then back to the right again breeze, with a swirl. Pin in the far right portion of the green.

The bunker was really in play.

Waymon was looking directly into thousands of eyes.

The super whopper was opening and closing its wings slowly, like a butterfly. The pulsating thorax was pulsating, sure, they do that all day, but the super whopper was moving its pulsating thorax around a lot, too, as if its thorax were searching for something important. Specifically, it was pushing its stinger down—and into—Waymon's mouth in hopes of finding the soft tongue of the human. It was sort of doing this like a cat does its tail. Working it. Real mean and sure and slow, like a cat does its tail right before it claws your eyeballs out of your head.

"Uncle!" Waymon squawked. "Get *off* me."

Albert Einstein snapped a couple of shots. The flagstick was in the background so it was going to make a nice photo, but of course his fingers were over the lens again so it wasn't going to make a nice photo.

Waymon also realized that this super whopper wasn't seven inches long as the May report of professor Biswapati's Ultimate! and Exclusive! Giant Cicada Killer Wasp web site had noted. This one was a little bigger than that. Therefore, Waymon, real worked up, suddenly began speaking in tongues. And because all of the people in the group had heretofore in their lives never heard a person speak in tongues, what Waymon said next in a tone of voice extremely particular to when a person speaks in tongues while he's being stung on the tongue by a mutate wasp, was slightly unnerving. "Hala-sha-mamba… Walla-mon-hal-som-ba-ta-ta!" Waymon yelped something to that effect as he pranced around the tee box on his tiptoes in circles.

"Hello, Tokyo," Mike said.

"Son of a *gun*," the Golden Bear said. "Will ya listen at *that*."

"Oh, *this* is quaint," the president said, rolling his eyes some more.

"Hey, fellows," the Golden Bear chirped.

"Yes, Golden Bear?" they all said in unison except Waymon.

"Waymon's talking *backwards*. *That's* what he's doing," the Golden Bear said like a kid. "I heard this woman on National Public Radio one time talk *backwards*. Then she sang the dang Pledge of Allegiance—*backwards*. Will ya just listen at *that*." The Golden Bear pointed at Waymon. "And one time I was up late after like the second round of the U. S. Open, watching Jay Leno, and he had that same woman on and she just starts in on 'Amazing

Grace,' but *backwards*. And she was just as normal looking as *anybody*. But there she was, just a-singing that wonderful song from back to front. I'll never forget it as long as I—"

"Golden Bear, you *dumb* ass. It's that *tongues* stuff," Mike said. "See, when people of certain religious affiliations get all emotionally riled up they start squawking this stuff. Can't understand a dang word of it. Saw it one time in a snake handling documentary. *Tongues*, my friends—I promise you."

The president said, "Okay, then. Since everybody's got a goddamn opinion on Waymon—Albert Einstein, what do you think?"

Albert Einstein didn't say anything. He waved goodbye at everybody, then ran off into the woods, missing the opportunity for Waymon to give him a big tip, which Waymon had been planning to do. Seventeen dollars.

"Birdie Train?" the president asked. "*Your* thoughts?"

Birdie Train decided not to say anything either. He threw the Golden Bear's golf bag onto the ground, waved at everybody, then ran off toward that little building over there behind by the eleventh green that you could see when Larry Mize hit that great chip to beat Greg Norman in the playoff. Birdie Train slipped and fell into the pond, then swam real fast across it and ran off into the woods behind Albert Einstein.

Now Waymon looked as if here were clogging.

Mike was now pointing at Waymon, which was rude and inappropriate for the particular situation Waymon was in. Mike was also cackling. Not pleasantly laughing or chuckling. Cackling.

The hot air balloon had caught one of those mysterious Golden Bell zephyrs and was now spinning like a carousel and the photographer was wildly buzzing away at the action at the tee box then Rae's Creek then the tee box at Golden Bell then through the woods at a foursome playing the ninth at Augusta Country Club and so on and so on and around and around.

Professor Biswapati, in a shiny silver fireman's coverall with some real funky looking goggles and his turban, and his flamethrower, and his beard which was smoking a little, started for them, shouting in Hindi, translated, which sounds exactly the same as in English: "Motor scooter! Motor scooter!" He got to about five yards from Waymon and pointed the business end of the flamethrower at Waymon's head and put his finger on the trigger. The nozzle of the flamethrower was dripping some fiery looking oil type stuff that was bright red and bright orange.

The president held up a hand. "As Chairman of the Entomology committee, I don't *think* so, amigo. Why not just get a butterfly net and capture it and study it. You thought of that? Sell some goddamn advertising on your web site. Huh, you ever thought of the butterfly—net—idea?"

Professor Biswapati wanted to shoot that thing so bad he was spitting and foaming. "No. Not really."

"Malooka-sistawa-boom-sola-ta-ta-ta... ta-*ta!*" or something very, very much like that... and still clogging. Waymon's eyes were coming together just like his second grade teacher said they would when he grew up. But they were coming together too fast and now they were crosseyed the other way.

"So why don't you go *get* you one. There's got to be a hobby shop somewhere in Augusta or the metro area I'm sure. Get the yellow pages from Betty Simpson." The president pointed up toward the clubhouse. "Note your mileage and any food and beverage, job-related related expenses and the club will be happy to reimburse you."

Professor Biswapati started moping that way. He flung his flamethrower to the ground. "*Pam!*"

In championship competition, the Golden Bear was religious about having no more than one swing thought while he swung. And he was an undisputed veteran of championship competition. Absolutely undisputed. Occasionally he'd have two swing thoughts during a championship competition swing, but when he did, one swing thought was real big so then the other swing thought had to be real little. He was religious about it. But even when a golf writer asked him after a round in the press conference if he ever had two swing thoughts during the round, the Golden Bear would clear his throat and drink some Gatorade instead of answering the question, or sometimes he'd just tell a story about Gary Player instead.

The super whopper finally found purchase in the soft flesh of Waymon's tongue, which Waymon had been violently flicking from side to side in hopes of avoiding the stinger part. Waymon now stood as stiff as a statue, feeling the claws of the super whopper tighten on his cheeks. Waymon suddenly thrust out his arms as if he were being crucified. He closed his eyes.

As the Golden Bear took The Lincoln Continental back like a baseball bat to smash the super whopper on Waymon's face, the Golden Bear had a total of fourteen swing thoughts pulsating through his mind. All he wanted to do was to whack the super whopper enough where it would fall off and go away and not also smash Waymon in the face and they could keep playing golf, but instead he smashed Waymon in the face real bad. "Darn it, Waymon. *Sorry.*"

Waymon crumpled to the turf as the green and yellow guts of the super whopper gushed down both sides of his face. And some other weird stuff.

"*Wow,*" Mike said.

"Seems we had... *no choice,*" the president said distantly, thinking that a shot to the middle of the twelfth green was the prudent tact today. Why mess with the bunker or come up short in the liquid?

The Golden Bear was once again gawking at the head of The Lincoln Continental as if the details on why he had fourteen swing thoughts going on instead of one real big one and one real little one were printed on the face of the club.

Waymon was now turning purple. Just then, Toby's hand, with a Marlboro Light between his fingers, thrust through the turf. Very tightly, Toby grabbed Waymon's ankle and yanked him into the humid burrow.

Where Screams Echo

Because the ambulance was bouncing around so much, the paramedic was having a hard time sticking the long, sharp intravenous needle into a nice blue vein on the top of Waymon's left hand. The paramedic would just about have it all lined up, then the ambulance would hit a pothole or a curb or swerve around a car and the needle would get shoved into one of Waymon's wrist or knuckle bones, or one time right there into the soft flesh between two knuckles real deep.

Waymon popped awake to find this going on and a clear plastic mask over his face helping to pump pure oxygen into him. "I had *tol'* myself," Waymon said with a swollen tongue, so it was real mushy sounding, "that I wasn't going to lay up at fifteen—and I didn't. Waymon Poodle, remember *this* sir"—wagging a finger—"did not lay *up*."

The paramedic gave Waymon a forced smile typical to paramedics who are trying to concentrate on something important such as the life of their patient. "That's great sir. Thank you."

"But you can go into the water behind the green, too. Yesser-*eee*. You sure can. It's been *done*."

"Is that a tricky hole?" the paramedic said. "Fif… teen?"

"Oh *yeah*. It's the final round death hole for so many invitees."

"Well ain't *that* something. A *death* hole. I had heard golf was a tough sport."

The ambulance turned into the emergency driveway of Columbia County Hospital. Waymon leaned up a little and looked at the sign. Underneath the name of the hospital was a street address: 1931. "Hey, you know nineteen thirty-one was a big year for golf?"

The president and the Golden Bear swerved in behind them in the president's Rolls Royce. A hubcap popped off and hit, right between the eyes, a guy sitting on a bus stop bench who'd just been released from the hospital.

Milt Limp and his photographer and that hot air balloon were already hovering over Columbia County Hospital. The photographer was taking shots of the hospital. Milt Limp was already typing the story in his mind…

And this was where the powers of Augusta National Golf Club brought the unfortunate, innocent, purple-faced guest. I saw the Golden Bear make the worst golf swing of his long, historic career… so bad it had law suit written all over it.

They wheeled Waymon into his own room in the emergency ward and about four people pounced on him and started looking at his tongue and his busted nose with little flashlights and started asking the paramedic a whole bunch of questions that included math and scientific words. So there was a lot of poking and prodding and squeezing and yakking going on.

And it echoed in Waymon's mind.

But he was at peace.

The president and the Golden Bear sort of tiptoed up behind everybody and started gawking. They were both really hoping Waymon wouldn't die. Again. They were convinced Waymon had died there on Golden Bell's tee box, until Mike, since he was a medical student, and even though he was studying to be a podiatrist, was asked, not too politely by the president of TrustTrust, to quit standing there cackling and pointing and give our very special guest Mr. Poodle mouth to mouth resuscitation as having crossed eyes and turning purple was a real indication he's not getting air.

Mike, even though he was new at caddying, exercised that innate ability given to people who decide to caddie at real nice golf clubs, to stand there with a blank expression on his face, for an abnormally long time if necessary, until his man handed over a bill, or bills, of some satisfying amount.

"Goddamn, *here,*" the president had said, handing him a two-dollar bill. "Now blow some life back into Waymon." The president had looked up the eleventh fairway to see if any other groups were behind them, watching his guest die. "This is embarrassing."

So Mike got to pull the dead carcass of the super whopper off Waymon's face. The super whopper had dug in there pretty good. It didn't come off so easily, and when it did it made a crunching sound. Then Mike placed his shaking lips onto Waymon's.

Waymon could see the president and the Golden Bear standing back there. "Nothing personal, Jack, baby," Waymon said to the Golden Bear. A nurse shoved Waymon's head back down.

"No of course it wasn't, Waymon," the Golden Bear said. "The Golden Bear should have hit you in the nose with the seven." The Golden Bear nudged the president in the ribs with his elbow and they both chuckled.

Uneasily, however.

Waymon said, "I promise not to tell anybody I beat you and made you think about giving up golf forever and giving away all of your clubs and balls to inner city children. I promise."

The Golden Bear gave Waymon a strange look. "Beat me?"

"*Jack*, baby. You quadruple-bogied eighteen, right?"

The Golden Bear looked at the president who shrugged his shoulders. "Uh, *yeah*," the Golden Bear said. "The Golden Bear couldn't get out of that… concession stand?"

"That's right. You were eating all the cheeseburgers. So I had a sixty-two and you had an eighty-nine, with a triple cheeseburger. So do you think Nick Price will call me from South Africa and Greg Norman from Australia to say way to go, Waymon?"

Just then the doctor who was fussing over Waymon turned around to see who was bothering Mr. Poodle. As far as he knew, the patient had been stung on the tongue by a mutate super whopper giant cicada killer wasp then smashed real hard on the proboscis by a Japanese-made prototype driver not yet available in stores and then lost consciousness and then did not breathe for a while and might have even been dead for ten or fifteen minutes and they had not played the rest of the holes at all.

So according to the rules of golf, no scores could be officially recorded, he was fairly sure. Plus, Mr. Poodle was sunburned quite a bit. When the doctor recognized who was behind him, like a lot of people, he immediately told the Golden Bear for some weird reason what he shot last Saturday with his foursome (a ninety-seven) and congratulated the Golden Bear on him quitting smoking a few years ago.

"Thanks," the Golden Bear said.

The doctor also told the Golden Bear that the next time he saw Arnold Palmer to tell him that he said he was glad he quit smoking, too. That the medical community was pretty sure now that smoking was bad for you.

"Will do," the Golden Bear said. "You got it."

Waymon said from his gurney, "And I'm so glad we found Toby, *too*. Toby sure did *smell*."

"Listen, gentlemen," the doctor said, "we've got to give Mr. Poodle a reality check so he can deal with his situation and help himself."

The president of TrustTrust said, "No we don't."

The doctor squinted at him, adjusted his glasses, then turned around and told Mr. Poodle the poop. It took a few minutes.

Then Waymon said, "So Nick Price isn't going to call me from South Africa and Greg Norman from Australia to say, 'Way to go, Waymon?'"

The president and the Golden Bear glanced at each other, then the president said, "I wish the good doctor hadn't *done* that." The president stood on his toes to get a good look at Waymon. "Hey, *Way*mon, you're not the... *liti*gious type, are you?"

Waymon thought he had said "religious" type, so Waymon said, supremely unequivocally, confidently, with a passion that rumbled up from down deep, "Yes, I am—sweet precious *Jeee*-sus."

"*Damn*." The president rubbed his chin. "And while we're at it, I'll bet you think we oughta let some ol' *wo*man in?"

Waymon thought the president asked, "And while we're at it, I'll bet you think we oughta let some healing begin?"

"This *in*stant, praise *Jeee*-sus. This *in*stant," Waymon said in a tone that was pretty much supremely unequivocal for the second time. "Oh, praise Jesus."

"Damn a-*gain*," the president said. We're in a real *fix* here, Golden Bear. I'm looking at double bogey."

"The Golden Bear knows what we need to do," the Golden Bear said.

The president said, "Ain't gonna happen, mister master. You've never had a double bogey. You don't know what it feels like."

The Golden Bear said flatly: "He saved your life."

The president pressed down the left sideburn of his toupee, which had been bent in an upward position in the Golden Bell fracas. "Just a little wasp. I was about to yank it off, ring its neck, you know, Golden Bear, by whipping it around and around like country women do when they're ready to eat a chicken, and hand it to my caddie."

"No you weren't." The Golden Bear gave the president a cool look, with one eyebrow raised. "Say, I think the Golden Bear can play any time the Golden Bear wants, *right*? I mean, *heck*, I've won the Masters six—"

"Yeah, six times. The president poked him in the chest again. "But you've never won the par three contest so maybe you're not such a master after *all*."

The Golden Bear gave the president an even cooler look than the earlier cooler look, this time with both eyebrows raised. "And the Golden Bear already has his own locker, right?"

"Sure. *Sure* you do. Your own locker. Big shit."

"And I can scoot right on through the front gate without anybody getting all upset, you know, once the guard sees it's the Golden Bear and I do my little wave."

"I will now alert our guards to shoot your tires out." The president of TrustTrust pulled his cell phone out of his pocket but it slipped out of his hand and broke apart on the emergency room floor.

They both watched the parts skittering around on the floor.

"And you're the new Membership Committee Chairman, right?" the Golden Bear asked.

"Uh, no, Golden Bear. I'm not even a member."

"Yes you are. You made such a big deal about it last night I almost puked and that would have been a darn good waste of some delicious lobster."

"They were really mutate crawfish. Like that goddamn mutate wasp. I'm surprised you haven't grown a third eyeball by now."

"May I continue?"

"No."

"And you said Waymon's the greatest teller in company history, right? Loves golf. Loves Augusta National Golf Club. Loves the Masters. Reigning Georgia State Amateur Champion. Six under as he stood on the tee of Golden Bell today, so that tells you something right there. So why not?"

"*Was* the greatest teller in company history. He got fired because all he thinks about all day is golf. So let's go. I want to go back and play some more."

"Six under. First time out. Waymon was on fire. And whatnot."

"I'm waiting for your point."

"Here's my *point*." The Golden Bear walked over to Waymon and put a hand on his shoulder and made some more golf history. "Waymon, what size jacket do you wear?"

Waymon reached into his mouth and pushed his swollen, purple tongue out of the way. "*Lawrrrge.*"

"No, Waymon. *Sport* blazer. You know—jacket. As in, you know, a *green* one like your Clemson *orange* one." The Golden Bear winked real hard, then smiled as if he'd won the par three contest.

Waymon reached back into his mouth and pushed his swollen, purple tongue out of the way again. "Forty-two... *lowng.*"

In Real Good Standing

Waymon Poodle was the new Executive Vice President of Customer Service of TrustTrust Banks, now making $978,000 per year instead of $12,250, with an amount of stock options that was downright socially and politically incorrect, a year-end bonus of no less than $1,000,500, and instead of driving a worn out Chrysler "Diplomat," zipping around Mullet Luv and the parking lot of Sans Souci real fast in a slightly pre-owned three hundred and seventy horsepower, eighty-two-thousand-dollar Jaguar XKR coupe, "Phoenix Red," whose interior does not smell of luxurious Connolly leather but of roasted garlic.

Now, more than ever, no human being on earth loves more than Waymon does the Masters, the golf course on which it's played, and the wonderful sport of golf in general, even though all those things recently happened. He wasn't necessarily interested in anything iniquitous anymore.

It's Monday morning, and Waymon, who almost played Augusta National Golf Club two days ago, had a satisfied expression on his face anyway, and enjoyed a life finally worth living. In a faraway place, screams no longer echoed. Waymon Poodle was a member, for free, of Augusta National Golf Club, and so was his fiancée, LaJuanita Mumps, for free, as all of the members of Augusta National Golf Club felt that adding a surprise announcement about LaJuanita's membership status in Waymon's new-member, 3-ring binder kit—which also included a monstrously detailed confidentiality agreement that was ten inches thick for Waymon and LaJuanita to sign—was a fantastic idea as they were super, super eager to please him and LaJuanita. The binder was delivered to Waymon in Mullet Luv in a Brinks truck. About forty guys with shotguns and dark aviator sunglasses and ear plugs jumped out and were not smiling and were looking around a lot with their fingers on the triggers.

And now Waymon made golf history yet again, this time in the kitchen of apartment number 1931 of Mullet Luv's Sans Souci apartment complex, and this time by being the person to tell LaJuanita Mumps of Mullet Luv, Georgia, that after all the recent ruckus in the wonderful world of golf, that she was the first woman ever accepted into the membership at Augusta

National Golf Club and that they had been sort of against doing it for over seventy years. Waymon told LaJuanita that she'd be the most famous woman in the wonderful world of golf for the rest of her life and have a lot of golf and fashion magazine articles written about her and the next time the phone rings it'll probably be that Oprah woman on TV wanting to interview you on her TV show. So congratulations, Waymon said shakily, and I love you. Waymon's head started to hurt real bad and a bad pain started up in his guts. Maybe it was really a bad pain in his soul he was feeling. He instantly regretted everything he just told LaJuanita. He sensed trouble as he looked at her. A Mullet Luv kind of trouble. Then Waymon added one more thing to what he sensed. He also sensed doom for his golf club. Doom, which was the most trouble a golf club could have, even over them wasps. He knew LaJuanita would eat that place up and probably get into a cat fight with that Oprah woman on her TV show if Oprah looked at LaJuanita the wrong way. Waymon gazed at what was squeezing out of her cheeseburger and oozing down between those big boobs. Waymon wondered why smart men made dumb decisions. But he was a smart man now. Very smart. One of them... they... those guys... us. Oh, Lord God Jesus. So Waymon started using his donkey smarts again. Waymon's expression, on purpose, was now as dull as a concrete cinder block. Even more impassive than a pile of beat up range balls.

LaJuanita had been standing there eating a Wendy's triple all the way with cheese, because she was real hungry. Quietly, she had also been appraising Waymon, but her expression was as dull as a concrete cinder block, too. Just as impassive as a pile of beat up range balls. Her very words were, delivered finally, and irritably, "Now, I don't wanna take no golf lessons. Every weekend I wanna go down there and I just wanna go play a couple of holes and then go eat and then go make love in one of those cabin things they got down there. Except we're going to have drinks with our food, too. They're called cocktails, Waymon. We're going to go get us some nice resort wear shit and look and act like fancy people once and for all." She poked the Wendy's triple at his face. "Don't screw this up." LaJuanita took another bite of the oozing triple, so vicious it made a crunching noise. Sure, the Mullet Luv Wendy's served fresh, crisp lettuce and pickles on their triples, but LaJuanita had big, dull-bottomed teeth that looked like concrete cinder blocks. When she ate a cheeseburger it was something to hear—and watch. "Waymon," she said, "you're creeping me totally out. What is it?"

"When did you learn about golf and golf lessons and where Augusta National Golf Club was and that they have cabins and all that?"

"You talk about golf and that goddamn golf club with yourself out loud in your sleep. Every night."

He had no idea. Now Waymon's donkey smarts told him to look real sympathetic at this point. Waymon made a real good sympathetic expression. "Sugar, I'm telling you, you won't like these fellows. All they do is play golf and talk about their score and whatnot in their snack shop."

"Like you do," she said. She took another chunk out of that cheeseburger.

"Well... and even though you're a smoking hot, foxy lady, they won't pay any attention to you. Not one bit."

She swallowed. "Like you do. Don't. Pay attention to me."

Waymon gazed at the slow moving ooze. He couldn't help it. He couldn't help but realize she had him figured out without much effort. He couldn't help but lean down and stick his tongue into her infinite cleavage and the ooze and start licking.

LaJuanita gently pulled his head even closer. Then she stuck her mouth into his right ear. Very loudly, she burp-talked, "Baby, come to... maaaaaa-maaaaaahhh."

Old Mrs. Willard Again

So Waymon's at his old window, the window in the middle, even though he doesn't have to do teller work any more, waiting on long-time customer Old Mrs. Willard, who, for the seven hundredth and twenty-third time, has brought in a check to cash for $250, given to her by her brother-in-law for something personal. Even though she saw Waymon back there in the branch manager's office busy talking to a real strange looking fellow, Old Mrs. Willard made a big fuss about Waymon coming out to his teller spot to give her his great customer service.

By order of the president of TrustTrust Banks, Waymon was to imme-diately find an exact copy of himself for the recent Mullet Luv Confederate Victory Parkway TrustTrust Publix branch teller opening. Then Waymon could come and start work in the big office downtown starting at 5:30 every morning until he retired. And he had to run in a bunch of mara-thons, starting Saturday in Iowa. So Waymon was interviewing his cousin, who was also named Waymon, who looked exactly similar to Waymon and had tremendous interpersonal skills, too. They were back there flapping their arms as they talked to each other.

And even though Waymon has waited on Old Mrs. Willard all those years, standing there wearing his Augusta National Golf Club tie, today was the first time she'd ever said anything about it, a tie everybody else usually noticed. She didn't even say anything about his nose, which was a mottled orange, green, and purple color. And a lot bigger than it normally was.

"Oh, *Waymon*," Old Mrs. Willard said while Waymon was flipping through the cash drawer, "so you're a member of the Masters?"

Waymon started to speak but his tongue got in the way.

"You know my oldest, Lucky, has always wanted to be a member of the Masters. Lucky told me he's heard it's real easy to get in if you act nice and know the right people."

Since his tongue was still swollen, but not quite as purple anymore, although it was still fairly purple, more turquoise than anything now, Waymon slowly, with sloth-like effort, told Old Mrs. Willard that a person isn't a member of the Masters... that that's the tournament... a person would be a member of Augusta National Golf Club... not the tournament... the Masters was the tournament they have down there at Augusta National Golf Club each year in April. Then Waymon did not make a huffing sound similar to the huffing sounds made by three-year-olds. He didn't even consider making a huffing sound, not one bit. Or a gurgling one.

Old Mrs. Willard didn't understood a single word he said. So to be polite she told Waymon that she'd go tell Lucky—since her next stop was to visit Lucky over at the county mental sanatorium—that Augusta National Golf Club was looking for new members. Then Old Mrs. Willard gave Waymon a nice wink.

Waymon gave her a wink back. A wink with deep meaning. A knowing wink, one that had some history, some real weight behind it, the best wink only a new member of Augusta National Golf Club could give without being found out he was a member of Augusta National Golf Club and getting in trouble with his new pals. Then Waymon handed Old Mrs. Willard exactly $250 in cash, and a big fat lollipop.

This time, a big fat green one.

Epilady

TWO MILES AWAY and a day later, LaJuanita had just done the Corn Cob on a mule. The hairdo looked like a six hundred dollar hairdo should look. And LaJuanita felt that any woman who paid for a Corn Cob should not be called a mule any more.

Now the valued customer was reclined on a squeaking plastic lounge chair in the back room next to the water heater with her legs spread real wide, waiting for LaJuanita to quickly—very, very, very, very quickly—yank the two wax strips that would violently wrench, from the roots of her very quivering and sensitive flesh, the untamed wads of hair that surrounded her thing. The customer was having herself prepared for a vacation to Myrtle Beach with her husband and his big golf buddy. She liked to ride along in the cart in her bikini thong. Only.

The customer reached over to the floor and picked up the newspaper and started reading it, but also deliberately used the newspaper to block from view the impending and horrifying scene developing between her legs, while smoking a Marlboro Light 100.

And it just so happened, as certain things were sort of doing a lot of in Mullet Luv lately, that the front page facing LaJuanita had a big, three-inch tall headline on it. So big it caught LaJuanita's eye. With her head cocked a little sideways, she read it. The headline blared, "AUGUSTA NATIONAL FINALLY BLOSSOMS." The subhead, two and a half inches tall, blared something else: "AND SHE'S GOT NICE CREDENTIALS."

LaJuanita read the story real quick. Everything it said about her was quoted by some man who ran the club named Huge Pecker. LaJuanita couldn't wait to get down there. Grinning iniquitously, LaJuanita yanked the wax strips... real... real... slow.

And all women screamed.

ABOUT THE AUTHOR

TODD SENTELL was born in Atlanta and raised in Georgia. For nine years he was the director of sales and marketing for an ootsie-tootsie private golf club. His comic fiction has appeared in *The Golfer*, *Atlanta GolfLife*, and *Orlando GolfLife*. His articles have appeared in *Atlanta Magazine*, *Dossier*, *Georgia Golf News*, *Golf Illustrated*, *Golf Georgia*, and the magazine of the Nationwide Championship, a former Senior PGA Tour event. He is a golfer, masters' level track athlete, and hardcore recreational boxer. He lives near Atlanta.

Provocative. Bold. Controversial.

The Game
A thriller by Derek Armstrong

Reality television becomes too real when a killer stalks the cast on America's number one live-broadcast reality show.
■ "A series to watch ... Armstrong injects the trope with new vigor." *Booklist*
US$ 24.95 | Pages 352, cloth hardcover
ISBN 978-1-60164-001-7 | EAN: 9781601640017
LCCN 2006930183

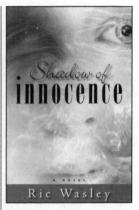

Rabid
A novel by T K Kenyon

A sexy, savvy, darkly funny tale of ambition, scandal, forbidden love and murder. Nothing is sacred. The graduate student, her professor, his wife, her priest: four brilliantly realized characters spin out of control in a world where science and religion are in constant conflict.
■ "Kenyon is definitely a keeper." STARRED REVIEW, *Booklist*
US$ 26.95
Pages 480, cloth hardcover
ISBN 978-1-60164-002-4
EAN 9781601640024
LCCN 2006930189

Whale Song
A novel by Cheryl Kaye Tardif

Whale Song is a haunting tale of change and choice. Cheryl Kaye Tardif's beloved novel—a "wonderful novel that will make a wonderful movie" according to *Writer's Digest*—asks the difficult question, which is the higher morality, love or law?
■ "Crowd-pleasing ... a big hit." *Booklist*
US$ 12.95
Pages 208, UNA trade paper
ISBN 978-1-60164-007-9
EAN 9781601640079
LCCN 2006930188

Shadow of Innocence
A mystery by Ric Wasley

The Thin Man meets *Pulp Fiction* in a unique mystery set amid the drugs-and-music scene of the sixties that touches on all our societal taboos. *Shadow of Innocence* has it all: adventure, sleuthing, drugs, sex, music and a perverse shadowy secret that threatens to tear apart a posh New England town.
US$ 24.95
Pages 304, cloth hardcover
ISBN 978-1-60164-006-2
EAN 9781601640062
LCCN 2006930187